Happiness rushed through her when she saw Caleb on the porch steps behind her.

Stop it! He was meant to be her twin sister's match and her way to happiness, not Annie's.

"Looks like you didn't get your laundry done earlier in the week."

"These are your cousin's and her *boppli*'s clothes."

"I didn't mean to dump this extra work on you, Annie. If you'd rather, I can pay you for taking care of my cousin and her *boppli* and find someone else to work with me at the bakery."

"No!"

His eyes widened at her vehemence.

She told herself to be cautious or she'd give away her true reason for accepting his job offer. Working with Caleb would be Annie's best opportunity to gently shove him and her sister toward each other.

"I want to work with you at the bakery," she replied as if it were the most important oath she could take.

And it was, because what she did while in Caleb's company could mean the difference between healing her sister's heart or not.

But what would it do to hers?

Jo Ann Brown has always loved stories with happily-ever-after endings. A former military officer, she is thrilled to have the chance to write stories about people falling in love. She is also a photographer and travels with her husband of more than thirty years to places where she can snap pictures. They have three children and live in Florida. Drop her a note at joannbrownbooks.com.

Books by Jo Ann Brown

Love Inspired

Amish Spinster Club

The Amish Suitor
The Amish Christmas Cowboy
The Amish Bachelor's Baby

Amish Hearts

Amish Homecoming
An Amish Match
His Amish Sweetheart
An Amish Reunion
A Ready-Made Amish Family
An Amish Proposal
An Amish Arrangement

Visit the Author Profile page at Harlequin.com for more titles.

The Amish Bachelor's Baby

Jo Ann Brown

HARLEQUIN® LOVE INSPIRED®

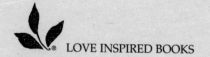 LOVE INSPIRED BOOKS

Recycling programs
for this product may
not exist in your area.

ISBN-13: 978-1-335-47901-3

The Amish Bachelor's Baby

Copyright © 2019 by Jo Ann Ferguson

www.Harlequin.com

Printed in U.S.A.

This is my commandment,
That ye love one another, as I have loved you.
—*John* 15:12

For Mike Freeman,
a superstar real estate agent…
with a fabulous sense of humor.
Thanks for everything!

Chapter One

Harmony Creek Hollow, New York

"Don't you dare eat those socks!"

Annie Wagler leaped off the back porch as the sock carousel soared on a gust and headed toward the pen where her twin sister's goats were watching her bring in the laundry. The plastic circle, which was over twelve inches in diameter, had been clipped to the clothesline. As she'd reached for it, the wind swept it away.

Snow crunched beneath her boots, and she ducked under the clothes that hung, frozen hard, on the line. She despised bringing in laundry during the winter and having to hang the clothing over an air-dryer rack inside until it thawed. She hated everything to do with laundry: washing it, hanging it, bringing it in and folding it, ironing it and mending it. Every part of the process was more difficult in the cold.

Pulling her black wool shawl closer, she ran toward the fenced-in area where Leanna's goats roamed. She wasn't sure why they'd want to be outside on such a frigid day, but they were clumped together near where Leanna would feed them later. Annie sometimes wondered if the goats were one part hair, hooves and eyes, and three parts stomach. They never seemed to be full.

And they would consider the cotton and wool socks a treat.

Annie yanked open the gate, making sure it was latched behind her before she ran to collect the sock carousel. She had to push curious goats aside in order to reach it. One goat was already bending to sample the airborne windfall.

"Socks are for feet, not for filling your bottomless stomachs," Annie scolded as she scooped up the socks that would have to be washed again.

The goats, in various patterns of white, black and brown, gave her both disgusted and hopeful glances. She wasn't sure why her identical twin, Leanna, liked the creatures, especially the stinky male.

Leanna had established a business selling milk and had begun experimenting with recipes for soap. Her twin hoped to sell bars at the Salem farmers market, about three miles southwest of their farm, when it reopened in the spring. As shy as her twin was, Annie wasn't sure how Leanna would handle interacting with customers.

They were mirror twins. Annie was right-handed, and Leanna left-handed. The cowlick that kept Annie's black hair from lying on her right temple was identical to Leanna's on the other side. They had matching birthmarks on their elbows, but on opposite arms. Their personalities were distinct, too. While Leanna seldom spoke up, Annie found it impossible to keep her opinions to herself.

How many times had she wished she was circumspect like her twin? For certain, too many times to count. Instead, she'd inherited her *grossmammi*'s plain-spoken ways.

Annie edged toward the gate, leaning forward so the socks were on the other side of the fence. She needed to finish bringing in the laundry so she could help her *grossmammi* and Leanna with supper. Her younger siblings were always hungry after school and work. She'd hoped their older brother, who lived past the barn, would bring his wife and *kinder* tonight, but his six-year-old son, Junior, was sick.

Keeping the sock carousel out of the goats' reach, she stretched to open the gate. One of the kids, a brown-and-white one her twin called Puddle, butted her, trying to get her attention.

Annie looked at the little goat. "If you weren't so cute, you'd be annoying, ain't so?"

"Do they talk to you when you talk to them?" asked a voice far deeper than her own.

In amazement, she looked up…and up…and up. Caleb Hartz was almost a foot taller than she was. Beneath his black broad-brimmed hat, his blond hair fell into eyes the color of early-summer grass. He had a ready smile and an easy, contagious enthusiasm.

And he was the man Leanna had her eye on.

Her sister hadn't said anything about being attracted to him, but Annie couldn't help noticing how tongue-tied Leanna was when he was nearby. He hadn't seemed to notice, and maybe Annie would have missed her sister's reactions if Annie didn't find herself a bit giddy when Caleb spoke to her. Before Caleb's sister, Miriam, had mentioned that Leanna seemed intrigued by her brother, Annie had been thinking…

No, it didn't matter. If Leanna had set her heart on him, Annie should remind him how *wunderbaar* her sister was. She'd do anything to have her sister happy again.

"Gute nammidaag," Annie said as she came out of the pen, being careful no goat slipped past her.

"Is it still afternoon?" He glanced toward the western horizon, where the sun touched the mountaintops.

"Barely," she laughed. "I've been catching up with chores before working on supper. Would you like to eat with us this evening?"

"Danki, but no." Caleb clasped his hands behind him.

Annie was puzzled. Why was he uncomfortable? Usually he chatted with everyone. While he traveled from church district to church district in several states, he'd met with each of the families now living in Harmony Creek Hollow and convinced them to join him in the new community in northern New York.

"What can we do for you?" she asked when he didn't add anything else.

"I wanted to talk to you about a project I'm getting started on."

Curiosity distracted her from how the icy wind sliced through her shawl, coat and bonnet. "What project?"

"I'm opening a bakery."

"You are?" She couldn't keep the surprise out of her voice.

A *bakery*? Amish men, as a rule, didn't spend much time in the kitchen, other than to eat. Their focus was on learning farm skills or being apprenticed to a trade.

"Ja," he said, then grimaced at another blast of frigid air. His coat was closed to the collar, where a scarf was edged with frost from his breath. "I stopped by to see if you'd be interested in working for me. The bakery will be out on the main road south of the turnoff for Harmony Creek Hollow."

She set the sock carousel on a barrel. "You want to hire me? To work in your bakery?"

"I've had some success selling bread and baked goods at the farmers market in Salem. Having a shop will allow me to sell year-round, but I can't be there every day and do my work at the farm." He shivered again, and she guessed he was eager for a quick answer so he could return to his buggy. "Miriam told me you'd do a *gut* job for me."

His sister, Miriam, was one of Annie's best friends, a member of what they jokingly called the Harmony Creek Spinsters' Club. Miriam hadn't mentioned anything about Caleb starting a business.

"It sounds intriguing," Annie said. "What would you expect me to do?"

"Tend the shop and handle customers. There would be some light cleaning."

"Will you expect me to do any baking? I'd want several days' warning if you're going to want me to do that."

He frowned, surprising her. It'd been a reasonable request, as she'd have to rearrange her household obligations around any extra baking. Asking Leanna would be silly. Her sister could burn air, and things that were supposed to be soft came out crunchy and vice versa. Nobody could quilt as beautifully as her twin, but the simplest tasks in the kitchen seemed to stump her.

"You've got a lot of questions," he said.

Don't ask too many questions. Don't make suggestions. She doubted Caleb would treat her as her former boyfriend had, deriding her ideas until he found one he liked so much he claimed it for his own.

His frown faded. "I may need you to help with baking sometimes."

"Will you expect me to do a daily accounting of sales?"

"*Ja.* Aren't you curious how much I'm paying you?"

She rubbed her chin with a gloved finger. "I assume it'll be a fair wage." She smiled. "You're not the sort of a man who'd take advantage of a neighbor."

His wind-buffed cheeks seemed to grow redder, and she realized her compliment had embarrassed him.

Apologizing would cause him more discomfort, so she said, "*Ja,* I'd be interested in the job."

"Then it's yours." His shoulders relaxed. "If you've got time now, I'll give you a tour of the bakery, and we can talk more about what I'd need you to do."

"*Gut.*" The wind buffeted her, almost knocking her from her feet as she reached to keep the sock carousel from sailing away again.

"Steady there." Caleb's broad hands curved along her shoulders, keeping her on her feet.

Sensation flowed out from his palms and riveted her, as sweet as maple syrup and, at the same time, as alarming as a fire siren.

"*Danki,*" she managed to whisper, but she wasn't sure he heard her as the wind rose again. It made her breathing sound strange.

"Are you okay?" he asked.

When she nodded, he lifted his hands away and the warmth vanished. The day seemed colder than before.

Somehow, she mumbled that she needed to let her twin know where she was going. He wrapped his arms around himself as another blast of wind struck them.

"Hurry...anna..." The wind swallowed the rest of his words as she rushed toward the house.

She halted in midstep.

Anna?

Had Caleb thought he was talking to her twin? She'd

clear everything up on their way to the bakery. She wanted the job. It was an answer to so many prayers, for God to let her find a way to help her sister be happy again, happy as Leanna had been before the man she loved married someone else without telling her.

Leanna was attracted to Caleb, and he'd be a fine match for her. Outgoing where her twin was quiet. A well-respected, handsome man whose *gut* looks would be the perfect foil for her twin's. But Leanna would be too shy to let Caleb know she was interested in him. That was where Annie could help.

God, danki *for giving me this chance to bring joy back to Leanna's life. I won't waste this opportunity You've brought to me.*

As she was sending up her grateful prayer and rushing to the house, she reminded herself of one vital thing. She must be careful not to let her own attraction to Caleb grow while they worked together.

That might be the hardest part of the job.

One task down, a hundred to go…before he started tomorrow's list.

Caleb glanced at the lead-gray sky as he moved closer to the heat box on the buggy's floor, shifting his feet under the wool blanket there. The clouds overhead were low. Snow threatened, and the dampness in the air added another layer of cold. He hoped the Wagler twin wouldn't remain in the house much longer. If he wanted to get home before the storm began, the trip to the bakery would have to be a quick one.

He hadn't been sure when he went over to the Wagler farm if he'd get a *ja* or a no to his job offer. He had to have someone to help at the bakery.

But is she Annie or Leanna?

He hadn't been sure which twin he was talking to. His usual way of telling them apart was that Annie talked more than Leanna, but without both being present, he hadn't known. Not that it mattered. He had to have someone help at the bakery because he had his farmwork, as well.

After almost two years of traveling and recruiting families for the Harmony Creek settlement, he finally could make his dream of opening a bakery come true. He'd turned over the community's leadership when the *Leit* ordained a minister and a deacon. It'd been the first service of the new year, and the right time to begin building the permanent leadership of their district.

He smiled in spite of the frigid wind as he glanced toward the white two-story farmhouse. Miriam had suggested he ask a Wagler twin to work for him. It had been a *gut* idea. The Wagler twins made heads—plain and *Englisch*—turn wherever they went. Not only were they identical with their sleek black hair, but they were lovely. The gentle curves of their cheekbones contrasted with their pert noses. Most important, they seemed to accept everyone as they were, not wanting to change them or belittle their dreams as Verba Tice had his.

His hands tightened on the reins, and his horse looked back as if to ask what was wrong. Caleb grimaced. It was stupid to think about the woman who'd ridiculed him. Verba was in Lancaster County, and he was far away. And...

He pushed the thoughts from his head as the back door opened and a bundled-up woman emerged. Her shawl flapped behind her as she hurried—with care, because there were slippery spots everywhere—to the buggy. He slid the door on the passenger side open, and she climbed in, closing it behind her. The momentary slap of wind had been as sharp as a paring knife.

"Sorry to be so long," she said from behind a thick blue scarf. "My *grossmammi* asked me to get some canned fruit from the cellar."

"It's fine." Which twin was sitting beside him? Too late, he realized he should have asked straightaway by the goats' pen.

How could he ask now?

Giving his brown horse, Dusty, a gentle slap of the reins, he turned the buggy and headed toward the road. He tried to think of something that would lead to a clue about which Wagler twin was half-hidden behind the scarf. He didn't want to talk about the weather. It was a grim subject in the midst of a March cold snap. What if he talked about the April auction to support the local volunteer fire department? The *Englisch* firefighters found it amusing when the plain volunteers called it a mud sale. He wondered if the ground would thaw enough to let the event live up to its name.

"Caleb?"

He wanted to cheer when she broke the silence. *"Ja?"*

"You know I'm *Annie* Wagler, ain't so?"

"Ja." He did now.

"I wanted to make sure, because people mix us up, and I didn't want you to think you had to give me the job if you'd intended to hire Leanna."

She *was* plainspoken. He prayed that would be *gut* in his shop, because he wasn't going to renege on his offer. It could be embarrassing for her, and him, and the thought of the humiliation he'd endured at Verba's hands stung.

And one thing hadn't changed: he needed help at the bakery. It shouldn't matter which twin worked for him.

Who are you trying to fool? nagged a tiny voice inside his head. The one that spoke up when he was trying to ignore his own thoughts.

Like thoughts of how right it had felt to put his hands on Annie's shoulders as he kept her from falling in the barnyard. He didn't want to recall how his heart had beat faster when her blue-green eyes had gazed up at him.

He must keep a barrier between him and any attractive woman. Getting beguiled as he had with Verba, who'd claimed to love him before she tried to change everything about him, would be stupid.

"Do you and your sister try to confuse people on purpose?" Caleb asked to force his thoughts aside.

"We did when we were *kinder*. Once we realized people couldn't tell us apart, we took advantage of it at school. I was better at arithmetic and Leanna excelled in spelling, so sometimes I'd go to the teacher to do Leanna's math problems as well as my own. She'd do the same with spelling."

"You cheated?"

"Not on written tests or desk work. Just when the teacher wasn't paying attention."

He laughed, "The other scholars never tattled on you?"

"They wouldn't get any of *Grossmammi*'s delicious cookies if they did."

"I didn't realize we had a pair of criminal masterminds in our midst."

"Very retired criminal masterminds." She smiled. "Our nice, neat plan didn't last long. A new teacher came when we were in fourth grade, and she kept much better track of us. Our days of posing as each other came to a quick end."

"So you had to learn to spell on your own?"

"And Leanna did her arithmetic problems. She realized she had a real aptitude for it and surpassed me the following year." Annie hesitated, then said, "I'm sure the whole thing was my idea. Leanna always went along with me."

He glanced at her. She was regarding him as if willing him to accept her words. He wondered why it mattered to her. For a moment, he sensed she was struggling with something big.

Again, he shut down his thoughts. Annie was his employee, and it'd be better to keep some distance between them.

"So you're now the better speller?" Caleb asked, glad his tone was light.

She laughed, "I don't know. We haven't had a spelling bee in a long time."

"Maybe we should have one. I read somewhere that *Englisch* pioneers used to hold spelling bees for entertainment." He gave her a grin. "Something we could do in our spare time."

"When we get some."

Miriam had told him how much fun she had with the Wagler twins, but he hadn't known Annie possessed a dry sense of humor. She wasn't trying to flirt with him, either, and he'd heard several of the community's bachelors saying Leanna was eager to marry. Maybe asking Annie instead of her twin hadn't been such a mistake after all.

When they reached the main road, Caleb held Dusty back. Traffic sped past. Most cars were headed to ski resorts in Vermont, and the drivers couldn't wait to reach the slopes. Local drivers complained tourists drove along the uneven, twisting country roads as if they were interstates.

Two minutes passed before Caleb felt safe to move onto the road. They didn't have to go far before he signaled a left turn. He held his breath as a car zipped by him, heading east, but he was able to make the turn before another vehicle, traveling as fast, roared toward Salem.

"Everyone's in a hurry," Annie said as she turned her head to watch the car vanish over abandoned railroad tracks.

"I hope they slow down before they get hurt." Pulling into the asphalt parking area behind the building where ghosts of painted lines were visible, he said, "Here we are."

"Your bakery is going to be here?"

"Ja." He was still amazed he'd been able to buy the building in October.

It had served as a supply depot for the railroad until the mid-1960s. The parking area and the pair of picture windows on the front were perfect for the shop he had in mind. Its wide eaves protected the doors. The building needed painting, but that had to wait for the weather to warm. As a few stray snowflakes wafted toward the ground, he couldn't help imagining how it'd look in May, when he planned to open.

"Why a bakery?" she asked.

"My *grossmammi* taught me to bake when I was young, and I enjoyed it." He didn't add he'd been recovering from an extended illness and had been too weak to play outside.

She glanced at him, and he suspected she wanted him to explain further. He didn't.

Walls. Keep up the walls, he reminded himself. Getting close was a one-way ticket to getting hurt again. He wasn't going to do something that *dumm* again.

Not ever.

The wind tore at Annie's coat and shawl when Caleb opened the door on his side and got out. When she reached for her door, he called to her. She had to strain to hear his voice over the wild wind.

"Head inside. Don't wait for me." He grabbed a wool blanket off the floor. "I'll tie up Dusty. I want to put this over him to keep him warm while I give you the nickel tour."

She nodded, but she wasn't sure if he saw the motion because he'd already turned to lash his horse to a hitching rail. The building would provide a windbreak for the horse.

After hurrying through the back door, she paused to cup her hands and blow on them. She wore heavy gloves, but her fingers felt as if they'd already frozen.

It was dusky inside. Large boxes were stacked throughout the cramped space. She wondered what was in them. Not supplies, because the room didn't look ready for use. Paint hung in loose strips between the pair of windows to her left.

She stood on tiptoe to look for writing on the closest box. She halted when she heard a quiet thump.

It came from beyond the crates. She peered around them. A door led into another room.

Was someone there?

Should she get Caleb?

A soft sound, like a gurgle or a gasp, was barely louder than her heartbeat. If someone was in trouble in the other room, she shouldn't hesitate.

God, guide me.

She took a single step toward the other room, keeping her hand on the wall and trying to avoid the big crates. Her eyes widened when she saw a silhouette backlit by a large window. She edged forward, then froze as a board creaked beneath her right foot.

The silhouette whirled. Something struck the floor. A flashlight! It splashed light around the space. A young woman was highlighted before she turned to rush past Annie.

"Wait!" Annie cried.

A *boppli*'s cry echoed through the building.

"Stop!" came a shout from behind Annie.

Caleb!

"There's someone here," she called as she spun, hoping to cut off the woman's escape.

She ran forward at the sound of two bodies hitting each other.

Caleb yelled, "Turn on the lights."

"Lights?"

"Switch…on the wall…by the door." He sounded as if he was struggling with someone.

She flipped the switch and gasped when she saw the person trying to escape from Caleb.

It was a teenage girl, holding a *boppli*. Blonde and cute, the girl had eyes the same dark green as Caleb's. The *boppli* held a bright blue bear close to his cheek and squinted at them in the bright light.

Annie started to ask a question, but Caleb beat her to it when he asked, "Becky Sue? What are you doing *here*?"

Chapter Two

Becky Sue?

Caleb knew this girl and the *boppli*?

Annie wondered why she was surprised. Caleb knew everyone who came to Harmony Creek Hollow. Was this young woman part of a new family joining their settlement? There was one empty farmstead along the twisting road beside the creek.

Annie faltered when she saw the shock on Caleb's face. His green eyes were open so wide she could see white around the irises, and his mouth gaped.

Then she remembered what he'd said after calling the girl by name.

What are you doing here?

He wasn't shocked to see Becky Sue. He was shocked she was in his bakery.

What was going on?

As if she'd asked that aloud, Caleb said in a taut tone, "Annie, this is my cousin, Becky Sue Hartz. She and her family have a farm a couple of districts away from where Miriam and I grew up." He closed his mouth, and his jaw worked with strong emotions.

The girl shared Caleb's coloring and his height. Annie wondered how alike they were in other ways.

Stepping forward with a smile, she tried to ignore the thick tension in the air. "I'm Annie Wagler. I should have guessed you were related to Caleb. You look alike."

"Hi, Annie." Becky Sue's eyes kept cutting toward Caleb. Her expression announced she expected to be berated at any second.

Why? For being in the bakery? It wasn't as if she'd broken in. The door had been unlocked. However, even if Becky Sue had jimmied a window and climbed in, her cousin would have forgiven her.

"And who is this cutie?" Annie tapped the nose of the little boy in the girl's arms, and he chuckled in a surprisingly deep tone.

For a moment, Becky Sue lost her hunted look and gave Annie a tentative smile. "This is Joey. He's my son."

Her son? The girl didn't look like much more than a *kind* herself. If Annie had to speculate, she would have guessed Becky Sue was sixteen or seventeen. At the most. The little boy, who had her flaxen hair, appeared to be almost a year old.

Shutting her mouth when she realized it had gaped open as Caleb's was, Annie struggled to keep her smile from falling away. Though it wasn't common, some plain girls got pregnant before marriage as *Englisch* ones did. Or had Becky Sue been a very young bride?

As if she'd cued Caleb, he asked, "Is your husband with you?"

Becky Sue raised her chin in a pose of defiance. A weak one, because her lips trembled, and Annie guessed she was trying to keep from crying.

"No," the girl replied, "because I don't have a husband. Just a son." When Caleb opened his mouth again, she hurried to add, "I'm not a widow, though that would be convenient for everyone, ain't so?"

"Everyone?" He frowned. "Do your parents know where you are?"

"Ja." When he continued to give her a stern look, she relented enough to say, "They know I left home."

"But not where you're going?"

She didn't answer.

"Where *are* you going?" Caleb persisted.

Again the girl was silent, her chin jutting out to show she wasn't going to let him intimidate her. Though the girl was terrified. Her shoulders shook, and her eyes glistened with unshed tears.

Knowing she should keep quiet because the matter was between Caleb and the girl, Annie couldn't halt herself from saying, "I'm sure you and Joey would like something warm to eat. It's cold here, ain't so? Though I was here last winter, I can't get used to it. Caleb, we need to get these two something warm to eat."

Caleb aimed his frown in her direction. She pretended she hadn't seen it. Didn't he understand they wouldn't get any information if the conversation dissolved into the two of them firing recriminations at each other? Once the girl and her *boppli* weren't cold and hungry—and exhausted, because Joey was knuckling his eyes with tiny fists and dark crescents shadowed his *mamm*'s eyes—Becky Sue might be willing to come clean about why she and her son were so far away from home.

But Annie's comments were ignored as Becky Sue said, "I told you, Caleb. I left home, and I'm—we're not going back."

"And you decided to come to Harmony Creek Hollow?" Annie asked, earning another scowl from Caleb.

"I heard about the new settlement." Though she answered Annie's question, she glared at her cousin. "I didn't know this was the one you were involved with, Caleb. If I had—"

"Well, isn't it a *wunderbaar* coincidence, Becky Sue?" Annie hurried to ask. "And your timing is perfect."

"It is?" Becky Sue seemed overwhelmed by Annie.

Gut! That was what Annie wanted. If the girl stopped thinking about defying Caleb, she might relax enough to reveal a smidgen of the truth; then Annie and Caleb could figure out what was going on.

No! Not Annie and Caleb. She shouldn't use their names together in her thoughts. *She* had to keep *her* focus on helping Caleb see what a *wunderbaar* wife Leanna would make him.

Wishing she could think of a way to bring her twin into the conversation, Annie said, "Your timing is great because Caleb was giving me a tour of his bakery."

"Bakery?" Hope sprang into the girl's voice. "I didn't see any food around here. Do you have some?"

"I've got soup in a thermos in the buggy." Caleb's face eased from its frown. "I meant to eat it for lunch, but I got busy and forgot."

"Wasn't that a blessing?" Annie hoped her laugh didn't sound as forced to them as it did to her.

"It probably won't be hot," Caleb said.

Annie frowned. Didn't he realize his cousin might be so hungry she wouldn't care what temperature the soup was? "We can heat it up."

He shook his head. "The stove isn't connected. Nothing is yet. The gas company is supposed to have some-one come later this week."

Annie made a quick motion with her fingers toward the door. Did he understand that she hoped, when he was gone, Becky Sue would open up to her? Sometimes it was easier to speak to a stranger.

The *boppli* wiggled in Becky Sue's arms and began crying. While the girl's attention was diverted, Annie gestured again to Caleb. He gave her a curt nod, but his frown returned as he headed for the door. If he disliked her idea, why was he going along with it?

Focus, she told herself.

Pasting on a smile, Annie held out her arms to Becky Sue. "Do you want me to hold him while you have something to eat?"

"No, I can do it myself." Her sharp voice suggested she'd made the argument a lot already.

With Becky Sue's parents? Other members of her family? Joey's *daed*? The girl had said she wasn't a widow, but where was the *boppli*'s *daed*?

Wanting to draw Becky Sue out without making the conversation feel like an interrogation, Annie began to talk about the weather again. Her attempts to convince the girl to join in were futile. Becky Sue refused to be lured into talking. Instead she stared at some spot over Annie's head as she bounced her son on her hip in an effort to calm him.

But Annie wasn't going to waste the opportunity. There was one topic any *mamm* would find hard to ignore. "Becky Sue, do you have enough supplies for your *boppli*?"

Her face crumbling as her defiance sifted away, Becky Sue shook her head. "I've only got one clean diaper left for him."

"Do you have bottles, or is he drinking from a cup?"

"I had a bottle." She stared at the floor. "It got lost a couple of days ago."

"My sister-in-law has a little one not too much older than Joey. I'm sure she or someone else will have extra diapers and bottles you can borrow."

Bright tears clung to Becky Sue's lashes but didn't fall. The girl's strong will astonished Annie. It was also a warning that Becky Sue, unless she decided to cooperate, would continue to avoid answering their questions.

"Gut," the girl replied.

"I know it's none of my business, but are you planning to stay here?"

"You're right. It's not any of your business." A flush rose up Becky Sue's cheeks, and Annie guessed she usually wasn't prickly. In a subdued tone, she added, "I don't know if I'm staying in Harmony Creek Hollow… beyond tonight."

"I'm glad you don't plan to go any farther tonight. It's going to be cold."

"I didn't expect the weather to be so bad."

"None of us did."

Annie watched as the girl began to relax. Becky Sue was willing to talk about trite topics, but the mere hint of any question that delved into why she was in Caleb's bakery made her close up tighter than a miser's wallet.

A few admiring queries about Joey brought a torrent of words from the girl, but they halted when the door opened and Caleb walked in. Annie kept her frustrated sigh to herself as she searched for a chair Caleb said was among the boxes.

Somehow they were going to have to convince the mulish girl to let them help. Becky Sue must be honest with them about what had brought her to northern

New York. Annie prayed for inspiration about how to persuade her to trust them.

Not having any ideas on how to solve a problem was a novel sensation.

And it was one she didn't like a bit.

While Becky Sue sat on the floor and began to feed her son small bites of the vegetable soup from the thermos, Caleb watched in silence. The same silence had greeted him when he came into the bakery. He'd heard Annie talking to his cousin, but Becky Sue had cut herself off in the middle of a word the moment she saw him.

Annie edged closer and offered him a kind smile. He was startled at the thought of how comforting it was to have her there. She was focused on what must be done instead of thinking about the implications of his cousin announcing the *boppli* was her son.

But the situation was taking its toll on her, as well. Lines of worry gouged her forehead. She was as upset as he was about his cousin.

"I'm sorry," he murmured.

"For what?" she returned as softly.

"Putting you in the middle of this mess. When I asked you to work for me, I didn't think we'd find my cousin hiding here." He gulped, then forced himself to continue. "Here with a *boppli*."

"You didn't know she was pregnant, ain't so?"

He moved out of the front room. When Becky Sue glanced at them with suspicion, he made sure no emotion was visible on his face. The *boppli* chirped his impatience, and she went back to feeding her son.

Standing where he could watch them, he leaned toward Annie. A whiff of some sweet fragrance, something that offered a tantalizing hint of spring, drifted from her hair. He hadn't thought of Annie Wagler as sweet. She was the forthright one, the one who spoke her mind. But standing close to her, he realized he might have been wrong to dismiss her as all business. She had a feminine side to her.

A very intriguing one.

"Caleb?" she prompted, and he realized he hadn't answered her.

Folding his arms over his coat, he said, "Nobody mentioned anything about Becky Sue having a *kind*."

"But you've got to let her family know she's here. She…"

Annie's voice trailed off, and Caleb looked over his shoulder to see Becky Sue getting to her feet. Annie didn't want his cousin to know they'd been talking about contacting Becky Sue's parents. A wise decision, because making the girl more intractable wouldn't gain them anything.

He realized Annie had guessed the same thing because she strolled into the front room and began asking how Becky Sue and Joey had liked their impromptu picnic.

The girl looked at her coat that was splattered with soup. "He liked it more than you'd guess from the spots on me. I should wash this out before the stains set."

Making sure his tone was conversational, Caleb pointed into the kitchen area and to the right. "The bathroom is through that door."

Becky Sue glanced at her drowsy son and hesitated.

Annie held out her hands. "I'll watch him while you wash up."

"Danki," the girl said as she placed the *boppli* in Annie's arms.

Becky Sue took one step, then paused. She half turned and appraised how Annie cuddled the little boy. Satisfied, she hurried into the bathroom and closed the door.

Annie began to walk the floor to soothe the uneasy *boppli*. He calmed in her arms when she paced from one end of the kitchen to the other. As he stretched out a small hand to touch her face, she said, "This may be the first moment she's had alone since they left home. I can't imagine having to take care of a *boppli* on my own while traveling aimlessly."

"What makes you think she's being aimless?"

"It seems as if she's thought more about running away than running to a specific place."

Caleb nodded at Annie's insightful remark. "We've got to figure out what to do."

"What's to figure out? She has to have a place to stay while you—" She gave a glance at the closed bathroom door. "While you make a few calls."

He was grateful she chose her words with care. If they spooked Becky Sue, she might take off again.

"That's true, but, Annie, I live by myself. I can't have her under my roof with nobody else there."

Puzzlement threaded across her brow. "Why not? She's your cousin."

"She's my second cousin."

Comprehension raced through Annie's worried eyes. Marriage between second cousins wasn't uncommon among plain folks. He had two friends who'd made such matches.

"Won't Miriam take them?" she asked, adjusting the *boppli*'s head as it wobbled at the same time he began to snore.

"Under normal circumstances, but she has caught whatever bug has made so many of her scholars sick.

When I stopped by earlier today, the whole family was barely able to get on their feet. She won't want to pass along the germs."

"Then there's only one solution."

"What's that?"

"She can stay at our house."

To say he was shocked would have been an understatement. "But they're not your problem."

She gave him a frown he guessed had daunted many others. He squared his shoulders before she realized how successful her expression nearly had been.

"Caleb, Becky Sue and Joey aren't a problem. Becky Sue is a girl *with* a problem. Not that this little one should be called a problem, either." Her face softened when she gazed at the sleeping *boppli* in her arms and rocked him.

He almost gasped, as he had when he recognized his cousin among the boxes in the bakery's kitchen. The unguarded warmth on Annie's face offered a view of her he'd never seen before. He wondered how many had, because she hid this gentle softness behind a quick wit and sharp tongue. He was discovering many aspects of her today. He couldn't help being curious about what else she kept concealed.

"We've got plenty of room in our house," she went on, her voice rising and falling with the motion of her arms as she rocked the *kind.* "There will always be someone there to help Becky Sue."

He couldn't argue. The twins' younger sister, Juanita, was in her final year of school. In addition, Annie's *grossmammi* and younger brother lived with them.

At that thought, he said, "You've already got your hands full."

"True, so we won't notice another couple of people in our house. Let us help you, Caleb. You've worked hard building our community, and doing this will give our family a chance to repay you."

Guilt suffused him, but he couldn't think of another solution. It seemed Becky Sue had already decided she could trust Annie. Now he must show he trusted her, too.

The bathroom door opened and Becky Sue emerged. When Annie asked her to stay with the Wagler family, she made the invitation sound spontaneous.

Caleb held his breath until his cousin said, *"Danki."*

"Get your things," he replied. "I turned the heater on in the buggy when I got the thermos. It's as warm in there as it's going to be, so bundle up. I'll stop by later and check on you."

"You aren't coming with us?" Becky Sue asked suspiciously.

"No. I've got work to do." Turning to Annie, he said with the best smile he could manage, "You taking them tonight will let me keep my work on schedule."

"Gut," Annie replied, as if the timetable for the bakery was the most important thing on their minds.

As soon as Becky Sue went into the front room, Caleb lowered his voice and said, *"Danki* for taking her home with you. Now I'll have the chance to contact her family."

"Do they have access to a phone?"

"I'm pretty sure they do. If not, I can try calling the store that's not far from where they live. The *Englisch* owner will deliver emergency messages." He couldn't keep from arching his brows. "I don't know what would constitute more of an emergency than a missing *kind* and *kins-kind.*"

"You know the number?"

"The phone here at the bakery is for dealing with vendors, but I've let a couple of our neighbors use it, and at least one of them mentioned calling the store. The number should be stored in the phone's list of outgoing calls."

Becky Sue returned with a pair of torn and dirty grocery bags in one hand. The girl carried a bright blue-and-yellow blanket in the other. Stains on it suggested she and her *boppli* had slept rough since leaving their home.

Joey woke as Annie was wrapping the blanket around him. He took one look at Caleb and began to cry at a volume Caleb hadn't imagined a little boy could make.

As Annie cooed to console him, she handed him to his *mamm*. She finished winding the blanket around him at the same time as she herded Becky Sue out of the bakery.

Caleb went to a window and watched them leave in his buggy. He went to the phone he kept on top of the rickety cabinet that must be as old as the building. He'd planned to start tearing the cupboard out after giving Annie a tour of the bakery. He wondered when he'd have time to finish.

Soon, he told himself. He'd set a date at the beginning of May to open the bakery. He'd already purchased ads in the local newspaper and the swap magazine delivered to every household in the area because his customers from the farmers market had been so insistent he inform them as soon as the bakery opened its doors.

Picking up the phone, he frowned when he began clicking through the list of outgoing calls. Someone had made a call about ten minutes before he and Annie had arrived. He had no doubt it was Becky Sue.

The number wasn't a Lancaster County one. It had a different area code, one he didn't recognize. He wasn't sure where 319 was, but he'd ask someone at the fire department where he was a volunteer firefighter to look it up for him.

But that had to wait. For now…

He found the number for the small store and punched it in. This wouldn't be an easy call.

Chapter Three

As Annie had expected, her arrival with Becky Sue and the *boppli* in tow threw the Wagler house into an uproar. The moment they walked in, her two sisters stopped their preparations for supper and came over to greet their unexpected guests. The family's new puppy, Penny, who was a hound and Irish setter mix Annie's younger brother had brought home the previous week, barked and bounced as if she had springs for legs.

Annie's efforts to catch Penny were worthless. The copper-colored pup was too eager to greet the newcomers to listen. Little Joey seemed as excited as the puppy. Becky Sue had to wrap him in both arms to keep him from escaping.

Annie pulled off her coat and tossed it over a nearby chair. She finally was able to grab Penny by the scruff. The puppy wore a mournful expression when Annie shut her in the laundry room. She hoped Penny would calm down at the sight of her dish filled with kibble.

Annie returned to the kitchen and looked around. A bolt of concern riveted her. *Grossmammi* Inez wasn't in the rocking chair by the living room door. Her *grossmammi* had lived with them for a year after Annie's *daed*

died from a long illness. When Annie's *mamm* married
her late husband's cousin and had two more *kinder*,
Annie had used any excuse to visit her *grossmammi*.

The elderly woman had taken them in a second time
after *Mamm* and her second husband, a hardworking man
who'd been a loving *daed* to his stepchildren, were killed
in a bus accident when Kenny was a toddler. Though
she couldn't do as much as she once had, *Grossmammi*
Inez supervised the kitchen she considered her domain.

"She's resting," Leanna said before she shot a smile
at Becky Sue and introduced herself.

Annie nodded, glad her twin knew what was on her
mind. However, her uneasiness didn't ebb. Her *grossmammi* sometimes took a nap, but Annie couldn't recall her ever staying in bed while meal preparations
were underway.

Her attention was drawn to her guests when Becky
Sue asked, "You are twins, ain't so?" The teenager
stared, wide-eyed, at Leanna before facing Annie. "You
look exactly alike."

Leanna said with a faint smile, "I'm a quarter inch
taller."

"Really?"

Leanna lifted her right foot. "Only when I'm wearing these sneakers."

Everyone, including Becky Sue, laughed, and Annie
wanted to hug her twin for putting the girl at ease.

"I've never met girl twins before," Becky Sue said.
"There were two pairs of boy twins in my school, but
no girls."

"No?" Annie laughed again. "Well, now you have."

Before Becky Sue could reply, Annie's younger sister, Juanita, edged around Leanna. She was a gangly
fourteen-year-old who was already three inches taller

than the twins and still growing, though Annie doubted she'd ever challenge Becky Sue's height. Juanita's light brown hair was so tightly curled it popped out around her *kapp* in hundreds of tiny coils. It was the bane of Juanita's existence, and nothing she'd tried had straightened it enough to keep the strands in place.

"Can I hold him?" Juanita held out her arms to the *boppli*.

Annie smiled at her younger sister. Juanita wavered between being a *kind* herself and becoming a young woman. It was shocking to realize Becky Sue couldn't have been much older than Juanita when she became pregnant. Annie's sister hadn't begun to attend youth events yet, preferring to spend time with girls her own age. They seemed more interested in besting the boys at sports than flirting.

"This is my sister Juanita," she explained to Becky Sue. "We've got two brothers, as well. Lyndon is married and lives next door, and Kenny, who's twelve, should be out in the barn milking with him. You'll meet him at supper."

Juanita cuddled Joey, who reached up to touch her face as he had Annie's. Becky Sue took off her coat and hung it up by the door as she scanned the large kitchen with cabinets along one wall and the refrigerator and stove on another.

Standing by the large table in the center, Annie smiled at her younger sister, who loved all young things. She delighted in taking care of the farm's animals, other than Leanna's goats and the dairy cows. She tended to the chickens, ducks and geese as well as the pigs and two sheep.

When Joey began fussing, Annie urged her sisters to return to making supper while she took Becky Sue upstairs and got her and the *boppli* settled. The extra bed was in Annie's room, but if Becky Sue was bothered by the arrangement, she didn't mention it. Annie cleared out the deepest drawer in her dresser and folded a quilt in it. Tucking a sheet around the quilt, she added a small blanket on top to make a bed for Joey. She urged her guests to rest while she went to help her sisters finish supper.

Annie asked Juanita to run next door to ask their sister-in-law if they could borrow some diapers and a couple of bottles for the *boppli*. Her younger sister was always happy for any excuse to visit her nephews and nieces.

Leanna didn't pause chopping vegetables for the stew simmering on the gas stove. Not that her twin would do any actual cooking. Juanita was already a more competent cook.

Hanging up the coat she'd draped over the kitchen chair, Annie went to the stove and checked the beef stew. She halted, her fingers inches from the spoon, as she wondered if Caleb would be joining them for supper. He'd said something about coming over after he called Becky Sue's parents.

"We need to set extra plates on the table," Annie said as she stirred the stew so it didn't stick.

"More than one?" Leanna looked up from the trio of carrots she had left to chop.

"Caleb said he'd stop over." Annie dropped her voice to a whisper to explain why he'd remained behind at the bakery. "It'll be a *gut* opportunity for us to get to know him better."

Her twin set down the knife and walked away from the counter. Taking the broom from its corner, she began to sweep the kitchen floor. "Why were you at the bakery today?"

"Caleb wants an assistant to help with getting it ready and to wait on customers when it opens. He asked me, though he thought he was asking you." She told Leanna about the conversation by the goats' pen. "If you'd like to take the job instead, I'm sure he'd agree."

Leanna stopped sweeping. "I've already got a job."

That was true. Leanna cleaned for several *Englisch* neighbors. She could have a house sparkling in less time than it took Annie to do a load of wash.

"This would be different." Her answer sounded lame even to Annie, but somehow she had to convince her sister to be honest about her feelings for Caleb.

Leanna was generous and kind and, other than her inability to cook and bake, something that shouldn't be as important to a man who owned a bakery, would make Caleb a *wunderbaar* wife. It was a fabulous plan, even if it broke Annie's own heart.

Frustration battered her. Why couldn't those two see what was obvious to Annie? Leanna and Caleb could make each other happy as husband and wife. Of that, she was certain.

Because you believe you *would be happy with him as his wife.*

Annie wished her conscience would remain silent. It was true she'd imagined walking out with Caleb before she noticed how her sister reacted each time he was near.

God, make me Your instrument in bringing happiness to Leanna, she prayed as she had so many times since her sister's heart was broken.

"It doesn't matter," Leanna said, "whether the job is different or not. I wouldn't have time to work for Caleb. This morning, I agreed to clean Mrs. Duchamps's house twice a week."

Annie recognized the name of one of the few *En-glischers* who lived along the meandering creek. Mrs. Duchamps had worked at the bank in Salem most of her adult life as well as taking care of her late husband during the years when he was ill. Having no *kinder* of her own, it was no surprise Mrs. Duchamps had hired Leanna to help.

"I didn't know you were looking for more houses to clean."

Leanna smiled. "I enjoy the work, so why not? And we could use the money. Kenny is growing so fast it seems as if he needs new shoes every other month. This works out for the best because I wouldn't want to work at Caleb's bakery." She began sweeping again. "Don't you think it's odd he wants to start a bakery at the same time he's trying to keep his farm going?"

"Not really." Annie recalled the light beaming from his eyes when he spoke about his plans for the bakery. It was a chance to make his dream a reality.

"Then it's a *gut* thing he asked you instead of me." Leanna shuddered. "I don't know what I'd say to his customers, and I'd get so nervous I'd end up dropping a tray of cookies."

"You navigate among your goats without stumbling. Even when you're milking them."

Leanna laughed, "Having them crowd around me hides a lot of my clumsiness. Besides, I'm sure you're going to have *wunderbaar* ideas to help Caleb."

"Maybe. Maybe not." Annie began to chop the rest of the carrots.

"You never used to hesitate sharing your ideas, Annie. I wish I had half of the ones you have."

"Ideas come when they come."

Ideas did always pop into her head. She used to speak them without hesitation, but that was before she'd started walking out with Rolan Plank three years ago. They hadn't lasted long as a couple. After a month, he'd started to scold her for speaking up. He chided her for what he'd called her silly ideas. Yet, after he'd dumped her, he'd taken one of her so-called silly ideas and let everyone think it was his own.

"Either way," Leanna said, "I'm glad you're working for Caleb instead of me."

"But you could have had a chance to get to know him better."

"True, but I'm sure you'll share many stories about your time with him." Leanna paused for a long moment, then added, "I didn't think we'd still be talking about jobs now. I assumed I'd be a wife and *mamm*, but that hasn't happened."

"It will when—"

"Don't tell me it's God's will whether I marry or not." Her twin kept moving, each motion sure and calm in comparison with her voice. "I've heard that too many times."

Annie paid no attention to her sister's words. Only to her heartbroken tone, and Annie's heart broke, as well. Her sister had fallen hard for Gabriel Miller before they moved from Lancaster County, but Gabriel had wedded someone else. In retrospect, Annie wasn't sure he'd been aware of Leanna's feelings. As far as Annie knew, her sister hadn't told him. Instead, she'd decided to let him pursue her as the heroes did the heroines in the romance novels Leanna loved to read.

In the months since they'd arrived at the settlement in Harmony Creek Hollow, her sister had begun to emerge from her self-imposed isolation. Being a member of the Harmony Creek Spinsters' Club with two of their friends had helped. Now their friends Miriam and Sarah were married. In fact, there had been three weddings at the end of the year, and while Leanna was thrilled for her friends, each ceremony had been a reminder of what she wanted and didn't have: a husband and a family of her own.

Annie scooped up the chopped carrots and dropped them into the stew. When Caleb had offered her the job—even if it'd appeared to be a mistake—God had opened a door for her to help her sister. She ignored the familiar twinge in her own heart as she tried to convince herself that persuading Caleb to walk out with her twin sister would be the best idea she'd ever had.

How was it possible the evening was growing colder by the second? Each breath Caleb took seemed to be more glacial than the one before. He hadn't thought it could get any more bitter, but with the sun setting, the very air felt as if it'd turned to ice. He guessed by the time he'd left the bakery, got home and milked his cows, the mercury must have dropped to ten degrees below zero. It would be worse by the time he got up in the morning. The idea of heading into his comfortable house and calling it a day had been tempting, but he couldn't cede his responsibility for his cousin and her *kind* to Annie. He'd told her he'd stop by, and he couldn't renege on the promise.

As he led Dusty toward the Waglers' barn so the horse could get out of the cold, Caleb glanced at the goats' pen. It was empty, and he guessed the goats were huddling inside their shed.

Smart goats. He smiled at the two words he'd never thought he would put together.

Caleb's shoulders ached by the time he walked to the house. Trying to halt the shivers rippling over him was foolish, because he couldn't relax against the cold. His body refused to keep from trying to keep the polar wind at bay.

He climbed up onto the porch and rapped on the door. The faint call from inside was all the invitation he needed to open it.

Taking one step inside the mudroom connecting the kitchen to the porch, he was almost bowled over by a reddish-brown ball of fur. A sharp command from the table didn't stop the excited puppy from welcoming him.

Kenny rushed into the mudroom to collect the dog. Caleb smiled his thanks to the dark-haired boy before shrugging off his coat. Watching Kenny try to get the puppy to behave with little success, Caleb wondered if the boy's shoulders grew broader every day. Kenny wasn't going to be tall, but he was going to be a sturdy adult. Hard work in the barn was giving him the strength of a man twice his age.

Caleb set his coat, scarf, gloves and hat on a chair by the door because the pegs were filled. He turned to walk into the kitchen and then stopped as he took in the sight of the families gathered around the table. Two families. The Waglers—Annie and her twin, as well as her *grossmammi*, sister and younger brother, who was sliding into his chair, holding on to the puppy—and two members of the Hartz family: his cousin and her son.

Yet they could have been a single family. No one acted disconcerted. One twin held Joey on her lap and offered him bites of her food while his cousin sat on the opposite side of the table between a girl close to her age and the other twin.

But which twin was which? He was embarrassed that he wasn't sure.

His discomfort was overtaken by distress. He hadn't

been able to reach Becky Sue's parents. He'd waited by the phone at the bakery for an hour, hoping for a call back. He'd left after that because his dairy herd got uncomfortable when he delayed the milking.

"*Komm* in…and join us," Inez said, motioning to him.

The elderly woman was shorter than the twins, and though her hair was gray and thinning, she had the same blue-green eyes. It was more than a physical resemblance, because she said what she thought, exactly as Annie did.

"*Komm*…in, Caleb," Inez urged again when he didn't move. She paused often as if having to catch her breath. "Sit…so we…can thank God…for our food…before… everything…is cold."

He entered the kitchen, which smelled of beef gravy and freshly baked bread. When his stomach rumbled, a reminder he'd skipped lunch, he was glad he was far enough away from the table so nobody would hear it. "You could have eaten without me."

"See?" piped up Kenny. "I told you he'd be okay with it."

"But…I wasn't." Inez's tone brooked no argument, and the boy didn't give her any as he bent to soothe the puppy, who was lunging to escape so it could greet Caleb as he neared the table. "Hurry. Join…us before hunger…makes Kenny forget…his manners again."

When the twin holding Joey—Caleb was almost certain she was Annie—flashed him a quick smile, he dampened his own. He admired how Inez spoke her mind. Not that she ever was cruel or critical of anyone, though she denounced what she saw as absurd ideas. She, as one of his fellow firefighters was fond of saying, called it as she saw it.

The only empty chair was at the end of the table. He sat there and nodded when Inez asked him to lead grace. He was the oldest man present, and it was his duty. As he bowed his head, his thoughts refused to focus on his gratitude for God guiding his young cousin to the bakery where she could be found. He was too aware of both twins sitting at the table.

If he mistook one for the other...

Annie had given him an easy way to avoid admitting he hadn't realized which twin he was asking to work for him, but he couldn't depend on that happening again.

He cleared his throat to signal the end of grace. As he raised his head, he was startled by an abrupt yearning he hadn't expected. A yearning for a life where he could sit with a family of his own at day's end. Several of his friends had married in November and December and stepped into the next phase of their lives. He was moving forward as well, but not in the same direction. Was he missing his chance to have a family?

There wasn't time for such thoughts. Between the farm and the bakery, he had too much work to do every day. The responsibilities of a family would require more of his nonexistent time. He'd made his choice, and he shouldn't second-guess himself.

Caleb took the bowl of fragrant stew. He spooned some onto his plate, then more when urged by Inez, who told him in her no-nonsense voice not to worry if he emptied the bowl because there was extra on the stove. When he sampled it, he was glad he'd listened to the old woman.

He focused on eating as conversation went on around him. He looked up when Inez spoke.

"Leanna...pass the basket...of rolls...to Caleb." Inez gave him a wink as she spoke with her usual interruptions.

Seeing how the twins glanced at her, he wondered what
her pauses to take a breath meant. "I've...never met a...
man who doesn't...have room for...another roll...or two."

"Especially with apple butter," he replied as he waited
to see which twin did as her *grossmammi* had asked.
When it wasn't the one holding Joey, he was relieved.
He'd guessed Annie was the twin bouncing the little boy
on her knee and keeping Joey entertained with pieces
of soft carrot she'd fished out of her stew. He watched,
amazed at how she kept the *kind* fed while she ate her
own supper. He was beginning to wonder if Annie was
gut at everything she did. She'd handled the touchy situation with Becky Sue with a skill he didn't possess.

"I'm not as out of practice as I thought," Annie said
with a laugh. Was she trying to put him at ease for
staring? That she might be able to discern his thoughts
was disquieting. "I used to feed Kenny this way when
he was little."

Kenny grumbled something, and Caleb swallowed
his chuckle. No boy on the verge of becoming a teenager wanted to be reminded about such things.

As the meal went on and Caleb had another generous serving of the delicious stew, laughter came from
the Waglers. But Becky Sue was reticent, and every
movement she made displayed exhaustion. He wondered when—and where—she'd last slept.

A quick prayer of gratitude for their food, their families and for shelter from the cold night ended the meal.
Leanna offered to help Becky Sue upstairs so she could
rest, and Inez took the *boppli* into the living room to
rock him until he became sleepy. Kenny wandered off
somewhere with the puppy he called Penny.

Annie began to clear the table, carrying the dishes to

the white farmhouse sink. "Did you get in touch with Becky Sue's parents?"

"No answer yet."

"As soon as they get the message, they'll call. I can't imagine how happy they'll be to discover their daughter and *kins-kind* are safe with you."

"With you, actually."

"We're happy to help." When he picked up his dishes, she said, "You don't have to clear the table. I know you've had a long day."

"No longer than yours."

"But I didn't have to milk," she laughed. "Lyndon, Kenny and Leanna milk every day, and Juanita will help sometimes. I always try to find somewhere else to be."

"Why? There's something *wunderbaar* about being in a warm barn and spending time with animals willing to share their bounty with us." He set the dishes by the sink. "For me, it's one of the clearest symbols of God's gifts to us."

She turned on the water and squirted dish detergent into the sink. "That's a much nicer way of looking at milking."

"But not your way?"

"Definitely not." She chuckled as she reached for the dishrag.

"You may have your mind changed one of these days."

"Don't hold your breath."

He smiled. Trust Annie Wagler not to withhold her opinion! It was one of the reasons his sister liked her, and working together at the bakery was going to be interesting. At least he wouldn't have to try to guess what she was thinking.

"So you prefer spending time with a *boppli* who spits

up on you rather than a nice, clean cow who gives you milk?"

"Spits up?" She glanced at the spots of orange on her black apron. "I didn't notice. Oh, well. It'll wash out," she laughed. "Joey should be glad he wanted to sit on my lap rather than Leanna's."

"Why?" He was curious how the little boy had figured out which twin was which. And a bit envious of the *kind*'s intuitive ability.

"Leanna prefers *boppli* goats to *boppli* humans because she spent most of her teen years babysitting for an *Englisch* family who had a ton of rules about their *kinder*. They insisted she carry the *boppli* in some sort of contraption that wrapped around her shoulders. Half the time when she came home, she was covered with formula because they believed she should feed the *boppli* in the getup."

"That's enough to put anyone off from *kinder*."

Annie flinched, surprising him before she went to the table to collect more dishes. "She won't feel that way about her own *bopplin*. She'll be a *wunderbaar mamm*, I know."

"But you'll never like milking?"

"Never!" She carried the other dishes to the sink.

"Don't you know you should never say never?"

"That sounds like a challenge."

"It might be."

"It's one you're guaranteed to lose. Cows and I agree we're better off having as little to do with each other as possible."

"You're going to make me prove that you're wrong."

"About what?" asked Inez as she came into the kitchen. She set Joey on the floor and pressed one hand to her chest. An odd wheezing sound came from her, and she sat in the closest chair.

Annie rushed to her side. "Are you okay, *Grossmammi*?"

"I guess I'm not as young as I used to be." She glanced at the *boppli*, who dropped to his belly. "Chasing a young one is a task for someone with fewer years on her than me. So, what you are going to prove our Annie wrong about, Caleb?"

"That milking is a pleasant chore," he replied, though he wondered how Inez had failed so fast.

Beside her chair, Annie looked worried, but she kept her voice light. "*That* is something he'll never prove to me. *Grossmammi*, I can finish up if you want to go to bed."

He thought Inez would protest it was too early, but she didn't. Coming to her feet, she said, "A *gut* idea. These old bones need extra rest to keep up with a *boppli*." Before he could say he'd make other arrangements for Becky Sue, she added, "Caleb, we're glad to have your cousin and her *kind* stay with us." She wagged a gnarled finger at him. "Such things should go unsaid among neighbors, ain't so?"

Again, as he bade Inez a *gut nacht*, he was discomfited at how the Wagler women seemed to gauge his thoughts.

At the very moment Inez closed the door to her bedroom beyond the kitchen, Joey began to crawl toward them on his belly. Caleb bent to pick up the little fellow, but froze when Joey let out a shriek. The *boppli* clenched his fists close to his sides as his face became a vivid red.

"What's wrong?" Caleb asked as he reached again for the *kind*.

With a screech that rang in Caleb's ears, Joey cringed away.

Annie scooped up the *boppli* and held him close as

she murmured. Joey's heartrending screams dissolved into soft, gulping sobs as he buried his face in her neck. She patted his back and made soothing sounds into his hair. When the *boppli* softened against her, she looked over his head toward Caleb.

Sympathy battled with dismay in her expressive eyes. Caleb had never guessed a mere look could convey such intense emotion. Or maybe it was as simple as the fact he felt sorry for the toddler, too.

Becky Sue burst into the kitchen, wearing a borrowed robe over a nightgown too short for her. Her hair was half-braided and her *kapp* was missing. "What's wrong with Joey?"

"I think he's overtired," Annie said. "*Bopplin* get strange notions in their heads when they're Joey's age. Some don't like men. Others fear dogs or cats or tiny bugs."

"Do you know why he's scared of men?" Caleb didn't want to admit how relieved he was Joey's antipathy wasn't aimed solely at him, because he'd always got along well with *kinder*.

Becky Sue shrugged. Or she tried to, but her shoulders must have been as stiff as his had been outside in the cold, because they curtailed the motion. Instead of answering him further, she hefted her son and walked away.

Caleb watched her climb the stairs at the front of the house and vanish along with the *boppli*. Her lack of answer told him plenty. She was hiding even more than he'd guessed.

Chapter Four

The soft chirp from the makeshift crib beneath the dormer window woke Annie two days later. Though the sun hadn't risen yet, she guessed it must be after 5:00 a.m. because lights glowed in the barn. Her brothers were already milking. They'd be ready for breakfast when they were done, so she should get started on her day.

She glanced at the extra bed between her and the window. Becky Sue was burrowed beneath the blankets, her knees drawn up under her and her rear end in the air, as if she were no older than her son who'd been in the same position when Annie checked on him last night.

The two had settled into the Waglers' home more easily than Annie had dared to hope. Last night, *Grossmammi* Inez had come into the bedroom to bid them a *gut nacht* and had asked pointed questions about Becky Sue's trip north. Their guest refused to share where she'd stayed during her journey from Lancaster County or how she'd traveled. While *Grossmammi* Inez didn't push, neither did she hide her annoyance. However, nobody asked why the girl said nothing about Joey's *daed*. It was as if the man didn't exist.

Becky Sue would learn keeping such secrets was futile in a household run by *Grossmammi* Inez. The elderly woman wouldn't be denied getting her way. She'd astounded everyone in the family when she announced she wanted to move with Annie and her siblings to New York. No arguments would persuade *Grossmammi* Inez to remain in the *dawdi haus*, where they had lived with her youngest son and daughter-in-law and their eight *kinder*. This drafty old farmhouse was now home, and Annie was glad they had enough room for Becky Sue and Joey.

Last night, when Caleb had again joined them for supper, Leanna hadn't said more than a handful of words, but Annie had seen her twin glance at him. Had he noticed, as well?

Annie chided herself. Why had she talked about Leanna staying away from other folks' *kinder*? She had to be cautious. Caleb might have mistaken her jest for the truth. If he wanted a family, why would he marry a woman who'd had her fill of *kinder*?

With a soft groan, Annie asked God to help her curb her tongue. By His bringing Caleb's cousin into their lives, He was offering Annie a chance to find the perfect way to open Caleb's and Leanna's eyes to what a great match they'd be. She couldn't mess that up.

She must remember that when the interrupted tour of the bakery resumed. It'd been postponed for a few days because of extra work Caleb had at his farm, so Annie had used the time to figure out some ways to point out, while he showed her around his bakery, Leanna's attributes.

Working to find joy and love for her sister was the best way to make herself happy, too. She had to believe that.

If only Caleb's face didn't keep wafting through her

mind along with the sound of his voice when he spoke of his bakery. She inserted Leanna into the image each time his face reappeared. Once she became accustomed to thinking of Caleb and Leanna as a unit, Annie would be able to squash her attraction to him.

That was how it worked, ain't so?

Pushing aside her thoughts as well as her blankets when Joey began to make soft sounds again, Annie rose and went to where the *boppli* was sitting up in the deep drawer. He regarded her, wide-eyed. She doubted he understood when she leaned close to him and put her finger to her lips. When he copied her motion and gave her a grin revealing his four tiny teeth, she hurried to dress.

Annie twisted her hair into place and secured it with the ease of a lifetime of practice and set her *kapp* on top of it. Joey continued to make cheerful sounds, each one making her move faster so Becky Sue could sleep.

Edging around the other bed, Annie scooped the *boppli* up. He needed to be changed, so before leaving the room, she grabbed clean clothes from the basket delivered by her sister-in-law. Annie closed the door behind them.

The little boy tugged at Annie's *kapp* strings as she carried him downstairs. Getting a towel from the bathroom, she spread it on the floor. She changed him and tossed the dirty clothes into the washer. Once breakfast was over, she'd do laundry for him and Becky Sue.

She grimaced as she thought of hanging clothes out on another freezing morning, but Becky Sue was too tall for any clothing in the house.

She was surprised when Joey began to pull himself on his belly across the floor. At his age, he should be crawling on hands and knees. Instead, he seemed content to belly crawl to where she'd left his blue teddy bear.

When the door opened and her brothers entered, Annie had Joey on her lap and was feeding him cereal and pieces of toast.

Lyndon's eyes lit up at the sight of the *boppli*. He was a doting *daed* who spent every moment he could with his own *kinder*.

"No!" Annie put up one hand to keep her brother away.

"Sorry." He looked at his barn coat that was worn and stained everywhere. "Rhoda keeps telling me I need to wash before I hug the *kinder* so she doesn't have to clean them up."

"It's not that. My little friend here is scared of men. He's thrown a hissy fit every time Caleb comes too close to him."

"But he likes me," Kenny announced as he reached for a piece of toast in the middle of the table.

"Goes to show there's no accounting for taste, ain't so?" teased Lyndon.

Kenny stuck out his tongue and grimaced, bringing a laugh from his siblings.

Cold billowed off her brothers, and Annie got up, balancing Joey on one hip, to pour *kaffi* for Lyndon as her older brother continued to joke with Kenny. She hurried to the table when Joey began to fuss. Handing him another piece of toast, she set the cup by Lyndon's right hand.

The food she put in front of her brothers vanished. They downed the oatmeal, toast and bacon she'd had waiting for them. She listened to their banter while her sisters made bleary-eyed entrances into the kitchen. Juanita offered to make eggs for anyone who wanted them, and Lyndon and Kenny raised their hands. They seemed to have bottomless pits inside them, because neither ever passed up food.

Grossmammi Inez was the last to rise, something that once would have been unthinkable. She smiled when Juanita placed scrambled eggs and toast in front of her. Leanna poured a cup of *kaffi* and set it next to her *grossmammi*'s plate.

"A soul could get accustomed to such service," the elderly woman said with a smile.

Annie laughed along with her siblings, but was bothered by the uneven pace of her *grossmammi*'s breathing. *Grossmammi* Inez insisted it was the aftereffects of the cold she'd had before Christmas. Annie hadn't argued, but was beginning to fear it was something more serious because *Grossmammi* Inez seemed to be getting worse rather than better.

Joey pushed away her hand holding another piece of toast topped with apple butter.

"Done, sweetie?" Annie asked Joey as she'd heard Becky Sue do at the end of each meal.

He nodded so seriously Lyndon chuckled.

Putting the *boppli* on the towel with a handful of the blocks sent over from her brother's house, she went to the sink to wash off her sticky hands. She filled a bowl with oatmeal for herself and carried it to the table. Adding brown sugar and cream skimmed off the top of the milk Kenny brought in every day from the barn, she kept an eye on the *boppli* as she bent her head to thank God for her food, her home and her family.

And for a little boy who was chewing on one of the blocks as if he could gnaw off one side of it. He held it near his face, ran his fingers over it and then put another section in his mouth as if he thought it might have a different taste.

I'm going to need a lot of help with this, Lord, she added before she raised her head again.

Lots and lots of help.

"No goats trying to eat your laundry today?"

At the question, Annie looked over her shoulder. A pulse of happiness rushed through her when she saw Caleb on the porch steps behind her. She didn't try to pretend it was because she could postpone hanging clothes while she spoke to him and found out what was in the small white box he held. Seeing his smile set off a low, long rumble within her, as if a distant thunderstorm hid on the other side of the mountains.

Stop it! He was meant to be Leanna's match and her way to happiness, not Annie's. How could Annie be content if her sister was lost in her grief at Gabriel Miller's betrayal?

"No wind today," she replied. "That means I don't have to chase the sock carousel across the yard."

"Looks like you didn't get your laundry done earlier in the week."

"These are the clothes Becky Sue and Joey had with them."

He came to stand beside her on the porch. "I didn't mean to dump this extra work on you, Annie." He paused, and she could tell he was giving consideration to a thought he'd been wrestling with. "Look. I know I offered you a job at the bakery, but if you'd rather, I can pay you for taking care of my cousin and her *boppli* and find someone else to help me at the bakery."

"No!"

His eyes widened at her vehemence.

Telling herself to be cautious or she'd give away her true reason for accepting his job offer, she reached for another tiny garment in the basket. At supper last night, Leanna had said less than a half-dozen words to Caleb. She hadn't greeted him, but she'd wished him *gut nacht*, and she'd told him *danki* when he passed something to her at the table.

Yet each time he spoke to her twin, Leanna flushed. Annie wondered how anyone could fail to see her sister had feelings for Caleb. They needed a gentle shove toward each other. Working with Caleb would be Annie's best opportunity to do that before he found someone else to wed.

"I want to work with you at the bakery," she replied as if it were the most important oath she could take.

And it was, because what she did while in Caleb's company could mean the difference between healing her sister's heart or not.

Caleb searched Annie's face, wanting to be sure she was being honest with him. Not that he had any reason to doubt her because she was the most forthright person in Harmony Creek Hollow. He wouldn't have to worry about her manipulating him as Verba had when she tried to convince him to follow her plans for them.

Verba had hated the idea he'd have a business where he wouldn't be around the farm all the time. He'd seen that as a sign she loved him and preferred they spent time together. But as their courtship had gone on, he'd begun to believe that what he'd considered affection was, instead, a determination to mold him into what she deemed would be the perfect husband.

Why was he thinking of Verba? Or marriage? He must concentrate on the reason that had brought him to the Waglers' farm beneath the hills lifting toward the Green Mountains a few miles to the east.

He looked at Annie. A faint wisp of wind tugged at her *kapp* strings beneath her black bonnet while it played with the edges of the shawl she'd secured around herself in two places with clothespins. Her cheeks were almost as red as the sky at sunset, but her eyes, which seemed to vary in color between green and blue, were warm.

"Are you certain you want to take on both jobs?" He hoped she was. Trying to find someone else for the bakery could set back his plans and he'd miss the opening day he'd be announcing in the ads he'd ordered.

"*Ja*, Caleb. I gave you my word I'd take the job at the bakery, and it's not as if I'm alone in helping Becky Sue and Joey."

"Miriam hopes to be on her feet by the end of the week, and she'll be glad to have them come to her house."

"A house that's undergoing so much renovation isn't the best place for a little *boppli* who puts everything in his mouth." She hooked another clothespin onto a small garment.

"You sound as if you want them to stay here."

"*Grossmammi* Inez has mentioned several times in the last couple of days how nice it is to have someone around while Juanita and Kenny are at school."

"Leanna—"

"Has jobs of her own. She cleans houses for some of our *Englisch* neighbors."

"I didn't know that." Again he thanked God for leading him to the correct twin to ask for help at the bakery.

Annie bent to pick up the empty laundry basket. Straightening, she grabbed the clothesline near the pulley on the porch post and pushed the clothing along its length toward a huge maple tree. She grimaced and braced her feet as she tried to give the line a bigger shove outward from the house.

"Let me help," he said.

"Danki." She handed him the empty basket and grasped the line with both hands.

He stared at the laundry basket, then laughed.

She paused and asked, "What's funny?"

"You. Me. I thought you'd let me push the clothes out for you."

"Oh." The color on her cheeks deepened.

He hadn't intended to put her to the blush with his comment. For a moment he was as flustered. He hadn't imagined candid Annie Wagler was ever embarrassed. He had to wonder what other assumptions he had of her that would be overturned in the weeks to come.

He began to apologize, but she cut him off. Motioning him toward the line, she stepped back as she told him that she'd appreciate his pushing the clothes out another few inches.

Feeling like the world's biggest *dummkopf*, he handed her the empty basket and pushed the line out as she'd asked.

"Would you like to come in and have something warm to drink?" Her *gut* spirits seemed to revive themselves when she added with twinkling eyes, "It's the least I can do when you've helped so much."

"Hey, I pushed the last of the clothes clear of the eaves."

"Something for which we'll be forever grateful." She edged past him and opened the door. "I doubt we'll ever be able to repay you for this, Caleb."

He laughed, the cold air searing his throat. *This* was the Annie he knew, and he hoped she would continue to be irrepressible when she worked at the bakery with him. Laughing would make the time pass faster and the hard work more fun.

Caleb was still chuckling after he'd hung up his coat in the mudroom. He watched as Annie set the laundry basket by the washing machine.

"Inez, it's always a pleasure to see you," he said when he went into the kitchen and set his white box, which was full of cookies, on the counter.

"Aren't you a charmer today?" She motioned at the chair next to hers.

He looked around before he took another step.

"Becky Sue and Joey are resting upstairs," Inez said, as if he'd announced his thoughts aloud. "You won't upset the *boppli* when he can't see you. Sit and tell me the news while it's quiet."

Caleb smiled, not at her words but at how Annie rolled her eyes out of her *grossmammi*'s view. He wanted to assure them he understood the importance of patience when dealing with Joey. He needed the same forbearance when speaking with Becky Sue, who changed the subject or ignored his questions whenever he spoke to her.

He settled himself into the chair while Annie made and served fragrant hot chocolate to the three of them. Inez kept up a steady chatter of the latest tidings. Though she'd asked him for news, she had more than he did. Not just from their settlement, but from families beyond Harmony Creek.

"You are as full of information as *The Budget*," Caleb said between sips of delicious hot chocolate.

"Much of it comes from the circle letter Annie has kept going for almost ten years. Her cousins are scattered from here to Colorado."

He looked toward where Annie was by the counter.

"I was hoping to work at the bakery tomorrow. Will you be able to come?"

"Ja." She opened a cupboard door, blocking his view of her face. "Are you starting early?"

"By seven."

"I'll be there."

"No, I meant I'd pick you up at around seven."

She turned, and he saw her astonishment. "You don't have to pick me up. It's not a long walk to the bakery."

"It's close to a mile, a long distance in this cold. I don't mind."

"Say *danki* to Caleb, Annie," said her *grossmammi* before she could reply. "You'll do neither of you any *gut* if you take a chill and sicken as I did last month."

"Danki, Caleb. Leanna will be happy she doesn't have to worry about me." She came to the table and held out a plate of the oatmeal-raisin cookies Caleb had brought with him along with some snickerdoodles. "Leanna worries about us. Her heart is big, and she always has room for one more."

He nodded as he took a snickerdoodle, then a second one as Inez raised her snowy brows. He'd sampled cookies from the Waglers' house before, and they always were delicious. A quick bite told him these were better than he remembered.

"Astounding!" He finished the cookie. "Is that molasses I taste?"

"Ja." Annie sat facing him. "I've tried making cookies with molasses and with honey. I like the molasses version best. I like using variations in old cookbooks."

"Both honey and molasses are *gut* ideas."

"Our Annie always has ideas," Inez interjected with a smile. "Most of them are *gut*."

Reaching for another cookie, he replied, "If your

other ideas are as tasty as this one, Annie, I hope you'll share them."

A pretty flush warmed Annie's cheeks again, and he realized his request had pleased her. Knowing he'd brought a soft smile to her pleased *him*. More than it should for a man who didn't want to get involved with a woman. He'd have to be on his guard, but later...after he'd learned the recipe from her. The cookies would be a popular addition at his bakery once it was open.

Chapter Five

Except for the bone-gnawing cold, the day was perfect. No clouds marred the bright blue sky. Sunshine glistened on the snow along the mountains, turning each into a huge multifaceted diamond. The creek was almost silent as it ran between the thickening sheets of ice reaching out from both banks. Traffic was busy on the main road. Again Caleb had to wait before it was safe to pull out.

As he steered his buggy around the tall snowbanks and into the parking lot of his bakery, Caleb wondered how everything could be the same as the last time he'd brought Annie to the old railroad depot…and how everything could be so different. He glanced at where she sat next to him.

Her face was shadowed by her black bonnet, but he could see enough to know she was as anxious as he was. Maybe more, because she was dealing with Becky Sue and Joey. This morning, when he'd stopped to give Annie a ride, he'd seen only the back of Becky Sue as she rushed out of the kitchen.

"We're not going to find someone else lurking in the bakery," he said.

"Promise?" She gave him a faint smile. "Leanna is helping take care of Joey today, but she won't be able to most days. The people she cleans for depend on her, and she doesn't want to let them down."

"I'd like to say *ja*, that I promise no surprises at the bakery."

"But stranger things have happened."

"Stranger than finding my cousin with a *boppli* in my bakery? I hope not!"

When she chuckled, he relaxed. He couldn't say why he'd felt on edge as they approached the old depot building. He didn't expect anyone would be inside. He'd installed locks on both doors. But he couldn't push aside his uneasiness. He hoped Annie would see something he hadn't. Something—anything!—to give them a clue why the girl had run away.

Annie had used the word *coincidence*, but Caleb wasn't ready to accept that the encounter had been accidental. Becky Sue had chosen to come north. She'd admitted she knew about a new settlement but asserted she hadn't known it was the one he organized. That didn't add up.

Maybe if he had a chance to talk—really talk, one-on-one—with his cousin, he'd be able to get to the bottom of the tangle of half-truths and evasions Becky Sue used to keep him from learning why she'd left home. But his cousin was careful never to be alone with him.

Not that he could get within a foot of her when she carried her son, because Joey became hysterical each time he came near. He didn't want to accuse Becky Sue of using her son as a shield to prevent Caleb from talking with her, but it sure felt that way.

Again he wanted to apologize to Annie for saddling her with his cousin and her *boppli*. He didn't, knowing

Annie would push aside his words as she had before. Each time she spoke of being glad to help another member of the *Leit*, guilt rushed through him. He'd given her and her family a huge responsibility, which they'd accepted. In the meantime, he hadn't managed to get in touch with Becky Sue's parents. He'd left messages twice a day. The answering machine he'd hooked in the bakery hadn't been activated once.

"Here we are," he said as he stopped the buggy by the hitching rail.

"You've got a sign." She pointed to the simple plank he'd painted with Hartz Bakery. Underneath that, it said Not Open Sundays.

He planned to add the hours of operation later and edge it with strips of wood. Once the frost left the ground, he'd set it in place in front of the bakery. "Figured it was something I could do now."

"*Gut* idea." Annie opened the door on her side before he could reach for his.

Stepping out, he threw the warmed blanket over Dusty. He patted his horse before motioning for Annie to follow him to the door. By the time he reached it, his fingers were stiff with the cold. He fumbled with the key. The new lock didn't seem to want to open, but he finally unlocked it and threw the door open. He stepped aside so Annie could go in first.

When he heard her sigh with pleasure as she stepped into the kitchen, he hurried after her and switched on the lights. They showed the dust and dirt, as well as the water stains on the ceiling. No matter. By the time the bakery opened, every inch of the building would have been cleaned and painted. He wanted to impress the health inspector with the cleanliness of his bakery.

The temperature inside was around fifty degrees but

felt as balmy as summer in comparison with the outdoors. He unbuttoned his coat, letting the warmth banish the chill seeping through him. He recoiled when an elbow almost hit his chest, and he realized Annie was unwinding her scarf. She must not realize how close they stood to each other.

He couldn't be unaware of her, however. There was something about her that drew his eyes whenever she was nearby. She was so full of life, always looking on the best side of every situation.

Why hadn't one of the single men in the settlement asked her to walk out with him? Were they focused, as Caleb was, on establishing a toehold in the hollow? No, that wasn't true. They'd had three weddings last fall, and he'd heard rumors of other relationships or seen people pairing off to share a ride or a walk home after church services.

But he'd never heard Annie's name mentioned or seen her leave with anyone other than her family. It shocked him that he'd taken such notice of her without his realizing.

Caleb shed his coat and hung it and his black wool hat on a rack where aprons and towels would be stored. He took her thick shawl and coat and placed them next to his. He tossed his gloves on the lone cupboard set against the wall. The rest of the storage units remained in boxes, waiting for him to install them.

Annie untied her bonnet and set it on top of a cardboard box as high as her waist. Looking around, she said, "You're going to have more cupboards than every kitchen combined along Harmony Creek."

"I bought the appliances and cupboards from the owner of Summerhays Stables, who'd planned to renovate the family's kitchen. When they put an ad in *The Penny Pincher*, I jumped at the chance."

Annie didn't seem as surprised as he'd been at the high-end quality of the gas stove and ovens as well as the massive refrigerator and matching freezer that would take up almost half of the large room. Like his sister, Annie counted Sarah Kuhns as a *gut* friend. Sarah had worked as a nanny in the Summerhayses' home until the end of the year, so Annie knew how fancy the *Englischers'* house was.

Caleb was astonished by how self-conscious he was to show Annie around the kitchen. So far, he'd fixed broken windows and cleaned out debris. Once cabinets were installed over the concrete floor and the appliances set in their proper places, he planned to paint the fly-speckled walls. With a new furnace in the cellar, it was no longer so damp and cold the paint would peel off the walls almost as soon as he put it up.

What would Annie think of his future shop? Would she come to see it as he did, with ovens heating the space and wondrous-smelling goodies waiting in simple glass cases out front? Could she imagine, as he did, a day when the bakery would be crowded with eager customers?

He discovered he was holding his breath in anticipation of her reaction and forced himself to draw air in and out.

"You've done a lot of thinking about this," Annie said.

"I have."

"I can't wait for Leanna to see it. She says our kitchen would be easier to work in if we got rid of the appliances, which are older than we are."

He smiled, glad she could envision what he'd planned. "I dream big, I guess."

"There's no sin in that. The *gut* Lord gave us the ability to find the best ways to walk the path He's given us." Without a pause, she asked, "What sort of counters are you planning to use here in the kitchen?"

As he explained why he'd chosen quartz over marble for the area where bread would be kneaded and dough rolled out, he was delighted to have such a responsive audience. She asked questions, some he hadn't considered, and he thought of Inez's comment about how Annie had lots of ideas.

He again urged her to share them. Changes to his bakery would be fine as long as she didn't try to change him, too. He'd had enough of that with Verba.

"*Komm* into the front room," Caleb said, motioning to the other room. "It's where customers will be served."

She paused in the doorway and rapped her knuckles against the wall. At the hollow sound, she said, "You might want to consider a pass-through window here. Your customers could speak to whoever's in the kitchen. That would allow for special requests or questions about ingredients. So many people must be careful about allergies or gluten."

"I like that idea, though I'd have to make sure the kitchen was kept extra neat and tidy."

"If you don't want customers to see bowls filled with dough or bread rising, you could put bifold shutters on the window." She moved so she could appraise the wall. "Add a sign saying whether the baker is available, and you'll have customers who feel free to ask questions."

"Watch your step," he warned when she turned to follow him to the center of the customer area.

It was a little larger than the kitchen, but unlike the

concrete in the other room, this space had wide, dusty floorboards. He grimaced at several that had warped to the point the nails had popped, making the floor treacherous to anyone not paying attention to where they walked.

"Those boards look as if they're trying to escape," Annie said.

"From what I've been told, this building has been empty for more than ten years since the feed store that was in here closed."

"What's that?" she asked, pointing to a square cut into the floor.

"It leads to the cellar. Nothing there but cobwebs. There were mice, but I think they're gone."

He expected her to shudder, as most women did when mice were mentioned. She simply nodded and walked to the large front windows. Each had a checkerboard of wooden mullions.

"Did you have to replace any of these?" she asked.

"About a half-dozen panes. The yard out front was overgrown. Kids with mischief on their minds wouldn't risk the briars to get close enough to break many windows. I finished getting rid of the last thorn thickets the day before the first hard frost hit." He leaned a shoulder against the wall where a poster for some old-fashioned power tool was flaking into oblivion. "I didn't want to come over here that day, but if I hadn't, I would have had to wait until spring to finish digging them up. That could have meant opening later than the first week of May."

"Your customers wouldn't have wanted to walk through an obstacle course of bushes." She toed another loose board. "Have you considered painting this floor? A simple pale tan. It wouldn't show dirt as much as a dark floor, and the paint would seal in any splinters, so you don't have to worry about little ones getting hurt if they're on their hands and knees."

"That's a *gut* idea."

She gave him a cheeky grin. "I try to have only *gut* ideas."

Not quite sure how to reply, he continued with his tour. "The display cases will be here by the door."

"What about over there?" she asked, pointing to the other side of the room.

Caleb shrugged. "I'm not sure. Maybe a display rack or something else. I haven't given it much thought."

"How about putting small tables and chairs there?"

"I hadn't thought about that."

"You should be able to find something. They don't have to match. What do the *Englischers* call the style with mismatched furniture? Leanna was talking about it the other day because one of the houses she cleans is decorated that way. Shabby something or other," she laughed. "Oh, I remember. Shabby chic. Didn't you have some small tables in the barn when you and Miriam lived there before your house was ready?"

"*Ja.* They'd have to be refinished before they could be used."

"Paint them instead. It's quicker and will add color to this space."

"Let me think about it. Having the tables and chairs will be *gut* in case someone wants to sit while they're waiting."

She frowned in thought. "Have you considered selling *kaffi*, too?"

"No."

"You should. *Englischers* like to have a cup when they're enjoying a sweet roll or a muffin. Plain folks do, too, from what I've seen at the farmers market and the hardware store. You've got enough parking space outside to let people linger here. They might buy more when they see what other people order. It's like free publicity, because nothing helps sell sweets like someone taking a bite and saying, 'That's delicious.'" She looked up at the ceiling where the beams laced together in a simple square pattern. "If you don't mind, I'd like to get Leanna's opinion on flavors of *kaffi*. She knows a lot about them because she's tried many different ones."

"All right."

"How about free samples? Have you considered that?"

"Samples of what?"

"You could have a product of the day. Maybe you decide to make apple-cider doughnuts. You could put the doughnut holes out as a free sample. If they go fast, you can make apple-cider doughnut holes the next day and sell them. You could expand your products."

"I could." Caleb's head reeled.

Inez had been right. Annie had lots of ideas. He wondered how anyone else would ever be expected to keep up with her rapid-fire thinking.

But she wasn't finished. Facing him, she asked, "Do you think your customers will be tourists or local folks?"

"I'm hoping to have both."

He wondered if she'd heard him as she surveyed the room again, her gaze lingering on the far wall. Walking over to it, she stretched out her arms as far as they could go.

Again he was amazed by how small she was. Her personality was so massive she seemed taller than he was. But she was shorter—the right height, if he were to draw her to his chest, that he could place his cheek against the top of her *kapp*. His heart thudded as he imagined how she'd feel in his arms.

"This wall is wide enough you could display a queen-sized quilt." She turned to him and smiled, her turquoise eyes alight with excitement. "Some shops in Pennsylvania take quilts on consignment."

"I know, but I'm not familiar with how it works."

"The shopkeepers in our area would keep thirty percent of what the quilt sells for, which could be a tidy sum when *Englischers* will spend close to a thousand dollars for homemade quilts."

"Do you quilt?" He tried to figure how she'd find time to work at his bakery, take care of her family—and his—and make quilts.

"I can, but I'm not great at it. However, Leanna is a clever seamstress and has a *gut* eye for the colors and patterns tourists look for." She smiled. "I'm grateful to her for doing most of our mending, as well. She can repair a rip and make it appear as if there never was any damage. Right now, she's finishing up a quilt she plans to donate to the mud sale for the fire department."

"I thought she preferred to spend her time with her goats."

"She enjoys them, especially feeding and milking the does."

"Speaking of milking, don't think I've forgotten the challenge you gave me."

"What challenge?"

"To convince you that you could like spending time doing barn chores."

She laughed, "That's not going to happen. Ask Leanna. She already agrees with you."

He didn't listen as she continued. How many times

had she mentioned her sister's name, lauding Leanna's skills and kindness? Was this her way of trying to convince him he'd been wrong not to accept Annie's offer to step aside when he'd hired her? No, she'd been insistent she wanted the job and her twin had other work.

Maybe he was imagining how often she brought Leanna's name into the conversation. He had enough complications on his hands. He didn't need more.

Annie looked at Caleb, who had stopped responding to her suggestions. Had she overstepped herself by mentioning Leanna as she shared ideas? Today had been the first chance she'd had to keep her twin in the conversation.

He'd been asking questions, and she'd thought her plan was working, but he'd become silent. She could see he was deep in thought. She halted what she was about to say next about having handiwork for sale in the bakery. Clamping her teeth over her lower lip, she struggled to hush the many ideas bouncing through her brain like helium balloons.

She didn't want to appear pushy by making too many suggestions. However, he'd invited her to share her ideas. Probably he hadn't realized how many she had. She had to learn to temper the number she offered at one time.

God, there must be a reason You put so many ideas in my head. Are You trying to help me help others, or are You giving me these ideas as a way to teach me a lesson? Do You want me to learn to hold my tongue, or do You want me to give voice to Your inspiration?

Since she'd been old enough to realize not everyone blurted out idea after idea in an effort to find a solution, she'd been asking those questions. The answers hadn't come to her. Ignoring her thoughts had made her miserable, though she'd been extra careful after being betrayed by her former boyfriend. Since then, she'd tried to limit what she said. She should have guessed the opportunity to give voice to them today would overwhelm Caleb.

"Of course," she said into the silence, "the bakery is yours, and you can do what you think best."

"I appreciate your suggestions, but let me think about them to see how they fit in with my plans." Not giving her a chance to respond, he added, "There's one more place to see. The utility room."

"It's not in the cellar, is it?"

His smile returned. "No. If the bakery's business grows, I may look into using the cellar, but not until it's clean. That'll be a huge job."

"I'm not volunteering to do it."

"Me neither," he laughed and motioned for her to follow him into the kitchen.

Caleb had a lighthearted side to him she hadn't seen often. His sister laughed and joked with her three friends in the Harmony Creek Spinsters' Club, but Caleb had had to deal with many important issues before he turned the leadership of the settlement over to their ordained leaders. That hadn't allowed him time to be anything but serious.

This Caleb Hartz was too appealing for her own *gut*. Instead of thinking how enticing his smile was and how his laugh made her feel as delighted as Joey with a new toy, she had to figure out a way for him to act like this when Leanna was with him. There had to be a way, and Annie was determined to find it.

Caleb showed her the cramped closet with shelves on one side and space for crates on the other. It barely had room for a person to stand inside it and select something off the shelves. Its outer wall had once been a sliding door opening to the railroad tracks, but it was nailed shut.

"It's a shame this is a closet," Annie said. "This old door would give extra character to the front room."

"I can move it there. I need to insulate in there, and putting in a regular wall would allow that." He flashed her another smile. "An excellent idea, Annie."

Her knees seemed to melt with the warmth of his expression. It was wrong to react like this if she wanted to make a match between him and her sister, but she couldn't stop the ripple of delight any more than she could have stopped a freight train on the tracks outside. When his gaze met hers, she wondered if she could remember how to breathe as time seemed to stutter to a standstill.

The moment shattered when the phone rang.

Caleb jumped to answer it, and she took a steadying breath. She held it as she waited to see if Becky Sue's family was calling.

"That's okay," he said, hanging up the phone. He sighed, disappointment lengthening his face. "Wrong number."

"Becky Sue's family will call."

"They should have by now."

"Maybe they didn't feel right leaving a message because they weren't sure who would hear it."

"Like Becky Sue?" He leaned against a crate, folding his arms over his chest. "I'd thought about that. A couple of the guys at the firehouse have offered to lend me a phone or let me use their number, so Becky Sue's folks can reach them at any time, day or night. I'd hate to miss their call because I'm not here. I spoke with

Eli, and he agreed that having the cell phone for that purpose would be all right, so I'm going to borrow one when I go to the firehouse for our meeting tonight." He walked toward the door. "That's all there is to see. Tomorrow we'll get to work."

Staying where she was, Annie asked, "Have you thought about taking Becky Sue and Joey home?"

"I have." He faced her. "We could get a bus out of Saratoga to take us most of the way, but I'm not sure if bringing her home would make matters better or worse."

"You think she'll run away again?"

"*Ja.* Don't you?"

Annie breathed out before saying, "I do. Whatever set her to fleeing this time may not have been resolved. We can't know until she decides to tell us why she left."

Reaching for her coat, he smiled. "And can you imagine a bus trip with a *boppli* who sounds like a fire siren whenever I get within three feet of him?"

"You could sit at one end of the bus and have them sit at the other."

He started to retort, then burst into laughter. When she joined in, she couldn't keep from noticing how nice their laughter sounded mixed together.

"That feels so *gut,*" he said. "Some days, I wonder if I've forgotten how to laugh."

"It's not that bad."

"No?"

"Not for you, at any rate. You don't have a recalcitrant teenager and a *boppli* who would like to be attached to my hem."

"Annie, I told you—"

"I was joking again," she said to halt him from apologizing for the Waglers taking in his cousin and her son. "Having them at the house isn't any trouble. Our house is always in chaos anyhow. If you ever get tired of peace and quiet, come over and get your fill of noise."

"I will." He held out her coat.

When she reached to take it, their fingers brushed. She was shocked when a powerful sensation sizzled along her skin as if his skin had set hers on fire. She held out her hand for her coat again, and he offered it to her at arm's length. Had he experienced the same unexpected spark?

She must erase the memory of that delightful feeling. How could she make a match for her sister if she was growing more attracted to Caleb every time they were together? She could ruin all their lives if she wasn't careful.

Chapter Six

Wishing for spring to hurry up and arrive so the sun would rise earlier in the morning, Annie lit the propane lamp in the kitchen before moving to the stove. She'd made breakfast every morning since they'd come to Harmony Creek, and the motions were automatic. Which was *gut* because she'd been up half the night. Joey was getting another tooth, and he wanted to make sure everyone knew how much pain he was suffering. He'd fallen asleep, exhausted, an hour before Annie had to get up.

After a week of trying to sleep in the same room with a fussy *kind* and dealing with his *mamm*, who was becoming more defiant as each day passed, Annie took each step as if sloshing through a knee-deep swamp. She measured out *kaffi* and mixed up batter for pancakes. Looking out the window, she saw the glass was etched with a delicate filigree of frost. The patterns reminded her of the ferns growing in the woods higher on the hill behind the barn.

Summer seemed forever away, but she pushed aside the depressing thought as she reminded herself of how many times she'd been able to introduce Leanna's name into her conversation with Caleb at the bakery yesterday. He'd been a bit taken aback by the multitude of ideas she'd offered him, but he'd listened to her as Rolan had refused to…or, at least, she'd thought Rolan had.

Banishing Rolan from her thoughts, she couldn't help smiling. Had Caleb noticed her twin sister was a common denominator in the suggestions Annie had made? Trying to be subtle was proving to be harder than she'd imagined. It was so tempting to come right out and tell him Leanna would be the perfect match for him, but she always bit back the words.

Exactly as she tried to dampen how she was drawn to him and how a picture of his strong, hewed face filled her mind whenever she didn't keep it buried deep in her mind. That he'd asked her for her ideas had pleased her, though she'd scolded herself for sharing them.

During breakfast, while she listened to her siblings discuss their upcoming day and watched as Becky Sue fed Joey, Annie's thoughts battered her skull. She checked that Juanita and Kenny took their lunches with them to school. She offered to feed the goats because her twin had overslept and didn't want to be late for work.

Grossmammi Inez asked Becky Sue to help her with changing the beds upstairs and dusting. The girl started to protest, but a single glance in Annie's direction shut her down. Did she think Annie would kick her out of the house if she didn't assist with the housework?

Annie smiled as she fed the goats. Becky Sue shouldn't worry about Annie rescinding her invitation. In the Wagler house, *Grossmammi* Inez was the person who would make such decisions, and Annie couldn't imagine her softhearted *grossmammi* turning out anyone.

Hurrying into the house, she glanced at the wall clock in the empty kitchen. She had almost half an hour before Caleb was arriving to pick her up for work. She'd have enough time to...

Annie stared at what had previously been an open space by the table. A dark brown wooden high chair! Where had it come from?

She got the answer when the front door opened, and the other two members of the Harmony Hollow Spinsters' Club, Miriam and Sarah, walked in. They were bundled up from head to foot and carried laundry baskets filled with folded clothes.

"What's this?" Annie asked.

"Becky Sue and her *boppli* have to have things to wear, so we decided to surprise you by sneaking in the front door." Miriam unwrapped her scarf to reveal a broad grin and bright green eyes so much like Caleb's.

"Before you go on, how is everyone at your house? Caleb said you were sick."

"We were, but we're getting back on our feet. Having something to do helps. Sarah and I have been doing a door-to-door collection." She set her basket on the table. "With several *kinder* a bit older than Joey here, there are plenty of things people were willing to loan you for his visit."

Red-haired Sarah, who was a full head shorter than blonde Miriam, grinned as she put a box on the floor in front of the sink and took her glasses off to wipe away the steam fogging them. "The Summerhays family had a bunch of clothing and toys to share, too. They always buy more than they need." She laughed, "I don't think that will ever change."

The *Englisch* family treated their former nanny as if she were one of them. They'd come to her wedding and always stepped up to help her or someone she knew. Annie was sure it'd been Sarah's suggestion that had led to Mr. and Mrs. Summerhays selling the appliances they'd bought for the canceled kitchen renovation to Caleb for his bakery.

Miriam pointed to the basket she'd brought in. "The bag on top is from the thrift shop by the old county courthouse in Salem. The clothing isn't plain, but a *boppli* can go through a lot of clothes some days. Nobody among the *Leit* is going to be upset if he wears *Englisch* overalls one day instead of plain ones. Those I spoke with hope *Mamm* and *boppli* feel welcome here so Becky Sue won't run away again."

"He does seem to drool on everything, so we go through a lot of clothing."

Sarah dug into another bag and pulled out a trio of bibs backed with plastic. "Try these. The younger Summerhays *kinder* had so many they never used these. They're brand-new and should keep Joey's shirts a bit drier."

"Please thank them for their generosity."

"I have. We're blessed to have such kind *Englisch* neighbors." She smiled at Miriam as she added, "They've volunteered to talk to other *Englischers* and ask them to drive more slowly through the hollow. I hope their words are heard before someone gets hurt."

That changed the topic of conversation. While Annie continued to unpack the *boppli* clothes and toys along with items for Becky Sue, she thanked God for the warm hearts in the community. She listened while her friends talked about the quandary with speeding cars along the twisting road. There had been several close calls, but so far nobody, either *Englisch* or plain, had been hurt. Annie prayed God would continue to look out for the foolish speeders and keep everyone, including other drivers, out of their paths.

Hearing footsteps behind her, Annie turned and waved to Becky Sue, who was carrying her son. "*Komm* and see what your cousin and Sarah have brought for you and Joey."

The girl took one look, burst into tears and crumpled to sit by the table as *Grossmammi* Inez came into the kitchen. She patted Becky Sue on the shoulder and nodded to Miriam and Sarah, a grateful smile rearranging the lines and crevices of her face.

"Now Annie won't have to look so sad about having to do laundry every day." Her *grossmammi*'s words brought laughs from her friends.

"I don't mind doing laundry," Becky Sue said through her tears. She rubbed them away after Miriam took Joey from her.

The little boy ran his fingers along Miriam's face and leaned into her as he had everyone but Caleb. He stuck a thumb in his mouth and relaxed against her.

Miriam smiled as she rested her cheek on his soft hair. "Offer to help Annie with the laundry, Becky Sue, and you'll have a friend for life."

"You don't like doing laundry?" The teenager acted as if she couldn't believe what she was saying.

Annie laughed, "I despise it."

"Then let me take over the chore." The girl dimpled as she handed her son a stuffed rabbit from the stack on the table. After he'd held it close to his face and rubbed his hands over it, he began to chew on one of its pink ears. "It's the least I can do to repay you for taking us in."

"You don't have to repay us, but I won't say no to help with laundry." Annie looked at her hands and said with an emoted moan, "You won't be chapped all winter long."

Everyone laughed, then thanked her when she suggested hot chocolate to her guests, and *Grossmammi* Inez whispered that there were marshmallows in the pantry. By the time Annie came back with the bag, the table was cleared and Miriam was sitting next to her cousin and bouncing the *boppli* on her knee.

Her *grossmammi* and Sarah had moved into the living room to stack the clothing and other supplies to make it easier to put them away. Annie guessed they were giving Miriam and Becky Sue a chance to speak in private.

Annie went to the stove and clattered the pot and cups so she couldn't overhear the conversation at the table. She hoped Caleb's sister would do a better job convincing Becky Sue to divulge the truth than either she or Caleb had.

"Is everyone ready for a treat?" Annie asked as she put the steaming cups on a tray and carried them toward the table. "Before anyone complains, I put the same number of marshmallows in each cup."

While everyone chuckled again, Miriam glanced at her and gave the slightest shake of her head as Becky Sue lifted cups off the tray.

Annie understood what Miriam hadn't said. Becky Sue had refused to share anything new with her cousin.

As Annie set the empty tray on the counter, she heard the rattle of wheels. She cut her eyes to the clock and realized Caleb must have arrived. She'd got so caught up in chatting with her friends that she hadn't noticed time scurrying past.

When she looked out, though, she didn't see Caleb's buggy. Instead a wagon was parked there. It wasn't Lyndon's, and the man stepping out of the driver's seat was so wrapped in scarves around his black wool hat and his coat of the same color that she couldn't guess which plain neighbor had arrived. He reached into the wagon bed and lifted out what appeared to be a section of stair railing or a gate. He turned toward the house.

She rushed to the door to open it and let the man inside. The merciless cold struck her like a fist, and she stepped aside.

"I didn't think it could get any colder" came Caleb's voice from beneath the layers of scarves.

He leaned the wooden piece against the wall before he stripped off his gloves and began to unwind the scarves. He draped each one over the chair at the foot of the table. He nodded to Sarah and his sister, who held Joey, before greeting *Grossmammi* Inez and his cousin.

"I don't remember it being this cold last winter," Annie said.

"I don't think it was." He gave a quick shudder. "I'll get the rest of the pieces once my fingers have thawed a bit."

"The rest of the pieces of what?"

"A crib."

"You found a crib for Joey?" She resisted the urge to throw her arms around him and thank him. The little boy might sleep better if he had a crib.

"*Ja.* Every *boppli* needs a sturdy crib."

"Where did you find it?" Miriam asked as she stood along with the others to study the section of railing. "It was the one thing we couldn't borrow. From the looks of the railing, it's never been used."

"Jeremiah had been hired to build it, but then no one ever came to pick it up. He said we might as well use it instead of have it sit there in his workshop taking up space."

Annie ran her fingers over the smooth, polished wood railing. The oak had been finished with a reddish-brown stain. Jeremiah, who lived next door to Caleb, was a skilled woodworker as well as a farmer.

"It's *wunderbaar*," Becky Sue crowed. "*Danki*, Caleb."

"Like I said, you can thank Jeremiah." He took a cup of hot chocolate from Annie, then looked at the *boppli*, who was staring at the crib and at him with a somber expression. "You'll find it more comfortable, little man, than a drawer, ain't so?" He bent toward the *kind*.

As he did every time Caleb got within a few feet of him, the *boppli* began to bellow. His voice seemed too big for his tiny frame, and thick tears rolled down his cheeks.

Silence dropped on the kitchen except for Joey's shrieks. Annie wished she had something to say, but as she looked from her friends' shocked faces to Becky Sue's pale features, she couldn't think of anything that wouldn't make matters worse. Then she saw Caleb's pain and wondered if there were any words that would ease the situation.

Caleb was acutely aware of Annie and his sister witnessing the unsettling scene. Though Annie had tried to reassure him that Joey's reaction was nothing but an idea the toddler had got into his head, Caleb wasn't certain. The *boppli*'s cries seemed to get louder each time Caleb approached him.

"I'll get the rest of the crib," he murmured.

Realizing he still held the cup of hot chocolate, he set it, untasted, on the table. His gaze was snagged by Annie's, and he wondered if he'd insulted her by not taking a sip. Seeing her sympathy, he realized she sensed how distressed he was. He wanted to thank her for being understanding, but hesitated to do so in front of the others. How could common words seem too intimate?

He rushed outside where the cold felt almost welcome…for a few seconds before it threatened to freeze his lungs. Grabbing the other pieces of the crib, he carried them into the house. On his final trip he brought the mattress, which he leaned against the wall.

"Lyndon will set it up later," Inez assured him when he offered to put the crib together. "Another nap in the drawer won't hurt Joey." She smiled at the other women. "God has blessed this community with many *gut* hearts."

He didn't look at the *boppli* as he picked up his scarves. He started to twist them into place, then paused as he glanced at where Annie stood, her fingers laced together in front of her.

Her cheeks became the same shade as her rose pink dress, and she lowered her eyes. Was she feeling unsettled as he was? Maybe she could explain to him why he was uncomfortable, as if he were the one keeping secrets instead of Becky Sue.

"I should go," he managed to say. "Annie, are you—"

"Get over to the bakery," Miriam replied. "I know you can't wait to get to work. We'll take care of things here."

He turned toward the door, then glanced at Annie in spite of his determination not to. She was supposed to work at the bakery with him today, but she might want to remain at the house to help with sorting out the largesse.

"We'll be fine," her *grossmammi* said, warning the old woman might be discerning more than either Annie or he wanted. "Go and do your job, Annie."

"Ja. Danki." She went to get her coat and bonnet.

"I'll see you later." She squeezed Miriam's and Sarah's arms as she edged past them.

Caleb held the door for her as they went outside, warning her to watch out for a patch of ice near the wagon. He put his fingertips on her elbow to guide her around it, and the day seemed far warmer until he drew his hand back again.

As she climbed into the wagon, he berated himself. How many times had he made the promise—which he'd asked God to witness—that he wasn't going to let another woman get in the way of his plans to make his dream come true? He couldn't let his plans fall by the wayside because Annie Wagler touched a part of his soul he'd never guessed existed.

"You could have stayed behind today," he said when they were seated side by side on the narrow plank seat.

"No, I said I'd work for you, and I can't play hooky anytime something *gut* happens at home." Her eyes crinkled in a smile. "This way *Grossmammi* Inez and Becky Sue can have time to go through the donations."

"Which she couldn't do when I'm around because Joey would be too upset."

"Give him some time, Caleb. Think of what that little one has gone through. Assuming your cousin lived at home from his birth until they left, he has endured some big upheavals in recent days."

"True, but are you prepared for the gossip?"

Her brows lowered. "What gossip?"

"As I was warned before I bought my farm, everyone knows everything about everyone in Salem." He chuckled. "There's not a person in the village who hasn't heard my sister went to the thrift store and bought as many clothes for a *boppli* as she could find and brought them to your farm."

"Those gossips have heard about Becky Sue and Joey already, so they won't be surprised."

"You're right." He took his eyes off the road and gave her a wink. "But you know as well as I do stories change when they're repeated, whether along the Amish grapevine or among the *Englischers*. Who knows what the tale might become?"

Annie smiled beneath her scarf, which was covered in frost where her breath had turned to ice on the wool. How kind of Caleb to try to make her feel better about leaving when he was upset by how Joey reacted to him! She had no idea how to help him, so she played along with his silliness.

"I know too well about how things get distorted," she said as he steered the wagon around a rut. Though riding in the open wagon was far colder than his buggy, she didn't want to complain. It would take time to un-hitch and rehitch his horse, time he wanted to spend at the bakery. Shoving down another shiver, she went on, "In my circle letter, sometimes I hear outrageous things that the writer believes is true."

"I'm sure the rest of you set her straight."

"We try to, but by the time the letter gets back to that person, the matter's been forgotten."

When he chuckled, she savored the sound. She'd met Caleb in the living room at *Onkel* Myron's house a little over a year ago. He'd laughed like that, too, with her family. He'd come to talk about his plans for a set-tlement in northern New York. Many of the younger people in their district couldn't afford a farm in ever more crowded Lancaster County. To the north, they would be able to purchase land and build a future for themselves and their *kinder*.

Lyndon had been enthusiastic. He'd been working at a meat-processing plant and had hated being stuck inside for most of each day. The opportunity to have a farm was too sweet for him to let it pass him by. He'd told Caleb he wanted to come before discussing it with his wife. Rhoda had been as excited about the prospect of having a farm of their own as Lyndon, and the *kinder* had looked forward to having their *daed* home throughout the day.

Annie had listened as well, delighted to see her brother look happy for the first time since he'd gone to work at the plant five years before. But then she'd noticed how her twin was more interested in Caleb than what he had to say. How Leanna's eyes had glowed when she gazed upon him! Annie hadn't seen such joy on her twin's face since the news had come of Gabriel Miller marrying someone else the previous week. From that point until Lyndon purchased land for them in Harmony Creek Hollow days later, Leanna hadn't talked of anything but Caleb's plans and how it was an opportunity for them to put the small inheritance left by their late parents into a farm that could provide them with a home of their own.

At that moment, a plan—one to help her sister— had blossomed in Annie's mind. She'd waited to see if Leanna would let Caleb know or if her twin had found someone else in the new settlement. Neither had happened, but when she concocted the idea, Annie hadn't guessed how she would be drawn to Caleb herself. She couldn't be happy if her sister was miserable, so she must…

"What did you say?" She realized Caleb had asked her a question while she was lost in her thoughts.

"I was wondering if Becky Sue has said anything

about anyone in Iowa." He stopped the wagon beside the bakery and jumped out.

"Not that I recall," she replied as he came around to her side and held up his arms to assist her.

She put her hands on his shoulders. Leaning forward as he guided her to the ground, she found her eyes too close to his as his thick scarves brushed against hers. Her lips tingled as she imagined them on his without the wool between them. His gaze shredded her defenses. What would she discover if she were brave enough to explore the depths that were the color of deep green shadows?

Then her feet were on the ground, jolting her enough to break the connection between them. She thanked God for the pulse of common sense that had come in time.

"Why are you asking about Iowa?" Annie asked, focusing again on the mysteries surrounding Becky Sue.

"The day we found her at the bakery and I left a message for her family, I noticed there was an earlier call made to a number in the 319 area code. When I checked with Q yesterday, he looked online and found out the area code is in Iowa."

Annie recognized the nickname for the Salem Volunteer Fire Department's assistant fire chief, Robert Quartermaine. Caleb and Q had worked together to bring plain men in as volunteers. It'd been vital to the fire department because many of their members worked out of town, and there might not be enough to answer the siren and fight a fire. Because the Amish men worked at home, they were almost always available to respond.

"You think Becky Sue called someone?" Annie asked as Caleb opened the door and they went into the bakery.

"Who else?" He began unwrapping his scarves.

"The door was unlocked. Anyone could have wandered in and discovered the phone was working."

"That's true. I'd hoped it would be a clue to where she was heading." His face fell as hope dimmed in his eyes.

She regretted being blunt. Putting her fingertips on his sleeve, she said, "And it may be, Caleb. I wanted you to consider alternatives, but I've been wrong before. Plenty of times."

She was filled with the icy memories of how she'd been wrong to trust Rolan. As before, she tried to remind herself it was better she'd learned the truth before she'd risked her heart. That didn't help. His betrayal had seared her.

And she would never betray her sister the same way. Annie had to put aside her attraction for Caleb and help him see Leanna was perfect for him. She had to figure out how.

Chapter Seven

"I've told you everything, Caleb!" Becky Sue stood with her hands on her hips and her chin lifted in the pose she took whenever Caleb tried to probe into the secrets she refused to share.

He'd invited her to visit the bakery that morning on the pretense that he wanted to show her the recent changes, but she'd seen right through him. During the drive from the Waglers' farm to the main road, she'd repeated the story she'd told him and Annie when they'd discovered her hiding in the building. Not a fact changed, which made him more suspicious. Had she memorized what she was going to say ahead of time?

Caleb doubted his young cousin had any idea how difficult it was to keep his frustration from bursting forth. Only Annie's urging for him to let Becky Sue open to him in her own time kept him from demanding that she be honest right then.

"I'm willing to listen without judging," he said. "Whenever you want to talk, let me know."

"I want to talk without every conversation being about Joey." Tears blossomed in her eyes.

He looked at her standing in the half-finished

kitchen. The appliances were connected and some of the cabinets hung. Supplies remained in crates, stacked almost to the ceiling. One wall was partially painted a fresh white, the project Annie had begun yesterday.

Among the large boxes and shining appliances, Becky Sue appeared so young, so vulnerable...so much in pain. Sympathy flooded him, and he nodded. Annie had been right. Becky Sue was deeply hurt and had left everything familiar in the hopes of escaping that pain. Pushing her further would only add to her grief.

"Not talking about Joey won't be easy," Caleb said, trying to make his voice sound carefree. "He does so many new things every day, and if you don't tell me about them, Annie does."

Becky Sue regarded him with suspicion. Did she think he was trying to coerce her into letting down her guard?

Ja, she did.

He sighed. If she mistrusted him so much, what hope was there of him convincing her to be honest? He wondered why she'd come to Harmony Creek Hollow. Maybe she'd thought he would welcome her and her son and ask no questions.

She'd miscalculated. And his curiosity was matched by Miriam's. His sister had asked him almost every time they spoke if he'd discovered the reason Becky Sue had traveled north from Pennsylvania, but Miriam hadn't got anything more from the girl.

"Annie doesn't focus every conversation on why I'm here and what I plan to do next," Becky Sue retorted, her hands fisted at her waist. "She treats me like a person instead of a problem."

He flinched, remembering how he'd used the same word to describe Becky Sue and how Annie had chided him. Could they both be right? Had he got so accustomed to dealing with challenge after challenge with the new settlement that he'd lost sight of how people were involved? If so, it was *gut* he'd stepped aside as the district's leader. The *Leit* had been blessed by the lot when Eli Troyer had been chosen as their new minister and Jeremiah Stoltzfus as their deacon.

"You're right," he said. When Becky Sue stared at him in shock, he added, "I do admit when I'm wrong."

"Not something everyone in our family does."

At her bitter tone, he wanted to ask her to be specific, but guessed she would see his questions as another attempt to get the truth from her.

"Well, I'm one who admits when he's wrong. To do otherwise chances putting me on the road to *hochmut*." He sighed. "But I wish Joey would give me a chance. It's unsettling to hear him scream whenever I come near."

"Stay away from him, and he won't cry."

Again he had to bite back what he wanted to say. If her words were an attempt to infuriate him, he wasn't going to play her game.

Instead he said, "True, but I'd hoped for a different solution."

"I've got to get going." She edged toward the door.

Opening the door, she was gone. A wave of cold washed into the bakery in the moment before the door closed again.

Caleb watched out the window as she climbed into his buggy. Slapping the reins on Dusty, she drove at a speed that made the back wheels bounce on the frozen ground. She hadn't asked if she could use his buggy, and he'd have to grab a ride home with Annie.

Glancing at the clock, he saw she should be arriving in about an hour. He'd arranged for her to drive herself that morning so he could have time with his cousin. Persuading Becky Sue to open up to him had failed.

He pushed away from the window as the buggy disappeared along the road. Jamming his hands into his pockets, he strode across the kitchen, maneuvering around the big boxes holding supplies.

Today, he had no interest in unpacking crates. He was making a mess of dealing with his cousin, and he wasn't sure what to do next. His self-doubts surged forward, eager to consume him.

Most of those doubts spoke to him in his ex's voice. Verba had insisted he give up his dream of opening a bakery, and she'd wanted to keep him under her thumb because she'd started dictating to whom he could speak and when.

Fool that he was, he hadn't seen the truth until she'd demanded he ignore one of his *gut* friends and sit with her at a youth event. He'd said he wanted to talk with his friend, and she'd flown into a rage. Embarrassed by the accusations filled with half-truths that she'd spewed in front of everyone gathered in the barn, he'd had his eyes opened.

So he'd set out to make his dreams come true. He'd found the fallow farms along Harmony Creek Hollow that would make homes for others who shared his longing to own property and farm it. Now that the settlement was thriving, he'd turned to building a bakery where he could use products from his farm and others'.

What now, Lord?

Instead of an answer deep in his heart, leading him in the right direction, he heard the clip-clop of hooves. He glanced out the window and saw a buggy coming to a stop.

Why had Becky Sue returned? Had something gone

wrong with the vehicle, or—and he prayed he was right—had she decided to be honest with him?

He reached for the knob, then froze when he saw Annie step out of the buggy. What was she doing here? She wasn't supposed to come until…

The wall clock chiming the hour startled him, and he realized Annie was on time. He'd spent the last hour lost in thought.

Wasted the last hour, his conscience reminded him. Instead of opening a box and wrestling out the contents so he could hang another cabinet in place to get him one step closer to being able to open his shop, he'd stewed about the past he couldn't change.

Annie breezed in along with another punch of cold air. She called a cheery greeting as she unwrapped her wool shawl. That he gave her no answer didn't seem to bother her because, as she hung the shawl, her heavy coat and her black bonnet up, she told him about Joey's latest antics.

Caleb's failure to laugh at her story seemed to cut through her chatter.

She halted in the middle of a sentence and stared at him before asking with her usual candor, "What's bothering you?"

"How little work I've got done today." It was the truth…or most of it.

"What would you like me to do?" She bustled across the kitchen to where she'd left off painting the previous day. "Keep going with the white? Or do you want this wall a different color? Customers will be able to see through the door to this wall. Maybe you'd like it to match or contrast with the color in the front section."

"Why?" For once, he was glad to let her keep talking. It would allow him to pretend his biggest worry was the color of the walls instead of the secrets his cousin was keeping from them.

She shrugged. "To pull their eyes toward the kitchen and the aromas emanating from it."

"I'll worry about those details after the bakery opens when I see if anyone comes to buy my goods."

Her eyes narrowed. "What's this depressing talk? Your bakery is going to be a success, Caleb."

"You sound sure."

"I am." She smiled, and the sunshine seemed to glitter more brightly on the snow. "You've considered the roadblocks for you and the bakery. You've mapped out the route you want to take."

"I thought I had until you made some excellent suggestions for things I hadn't considered."

Annie tried to ignore the warmth of his compliment washing over her and figure out what was bothering him, but it was impossible.

Caleb thought at least some of her ideas were *gut*. Did that mean he wanted her to keep offering them? Should she ask?

In the moment of her hesitation, he went on, "Don't ever get the idea I don't want to hear your ideas. I can't promise I'll agree with them or do anything with them."

"I appreciate your honesty."

"And I appreciate yours."

Her stiff shoulders sagged as she let her anxiety sift away. He was open to listening to her ideas. Even so, she shouldn't verbalize every thought in her head.

Yet she couldn't help herself from replying, "If you appreciate my honesty, tell me *honestly* what's going on with you. I don't know if I've ever heard you sound so glum."

While he explained his futile attempts to get to the

truth of why his cousin had appeared in his bakery, she prayed again for the right words to remind him that everything that happened was in God's hands. In his frustration, he was forgetting that the One who knew everything wanted Becky Sue and Joey safe, too.

"I'm sorry."

"Don't be. Maybe by seeing how close your family is, Becky Sue will begin to miss her own enough to want to return home."

She laughed in spite of the tension lingering in the kitchen. "I don't know if she'll be able to pull Joey away from Penny. That *boppli* and puppy are never more than inches apart."

"Let's handle that obstacle when we get to it." He moved to a half-opened crate. As he bent to tear the cardboard away, he said, "*Danki* for listening to my troubles." He gave her an uneven smile. "*Danki* for listening to them again, I should say."

"I wish I could do more."

"You're doing more than you can guess. It should be our way to listen to each other and to learn from each other. Not just in our faith, but in the ways we decide to make our way while on this earth."

She pulled an extralarge shirt that had belonged to Lyndon over her clothes before reaching to reopen the paint can. "People are right, Caleb, when they say they know you would have done a *gut* job for us if your name had been drawn in the lot for minister or for deacon."

"It's time for others to lead the settlement."

"You don't miss it?"

When he didn't give her a quick answer, she perceived that, for Caleb, choosing whether or not to lead the settlement was a more complicated decision than she'd imagined. And why wouldn't it be? The settlement was something he'd worked very hard for, sacrificing his time and dreams to bring it to fruition.

"Ja," he replied, "there are times when I miss being involved. There are plenty of other days when I thank God for giving me time to build my business and to allow me to spend time studying His word so I may grow closer to Him." He sighed. "And ask His advice on how to help Becky Sue and Joey. She's a stubborn *kind*."

Pouring white paint into the roller tray, Annie glanced over her shoulder for a brief second. "She may seem like a *kind* to you, Caleb, but she's been thrust into adulthood by becoming a *mamm*."

"That doesn't mean she can withhold basic information from me when I'm trying to help her."

"Would you reveal everything you've experienced if she asked you to be honest with her?"

"It's not the same. I'm not a single parent who won't identify the other parent."

"We all have parts of our pasts we don't want to talk about." She selected each word with care, not wanting to turn his curiosity from Becky Sue to her. "She came to you."

"She said she didn't know this was the settlement I'd worked to build."

Annie grimaced as she picked up her roller and ran it in the tray. "You believe that thin tale? I might have believed it if she'd showed up on our doorstep or on the Troyers', but she looked for sanctuary in your bakery. Anyone in the area could have told her what this building was and who owned it."

"I didn't think of that."

"Neither did I. Not at first, but once my shock at her arrival wore off, I started to notice how she seems to know more about our settlement than she would have if she wandered into it by chance." She began to run the roller along the wall. "Have you heard anything from her parents?"

"Nothing."

"That's odd."

He wrestled the cabinet into place in an empty spot between the stove and refrigerator before he answered. "I think it's strange, too. Maybe I'd understand it if she'd be honest with me, but I'm getting nowhere with her."

"I knew that before you told me about your conversation with her this morning."

His brows pinched the skin over his nose as he frowned. "You did?"

"Of course. I'd have to be as unobservant as an infant not to notice how often you've tried to turn the conversation to the *boppli*'s *daed* and how every time Becky Sue has deflected your questions."

"Will you talk to her?"

"Me?" Her voice came out in a squeak as she paused with the roller against the wall. "But she barely knows me." Feeling paint trickle onto her hand, she moved the roller over the stream before setting it in the tray.

"She knows you better than she knows me. Will you help?"

"All right."

"All right?" He leaned against the cupboard as he faced her.

Breathing seemed as difficult as if she were under the clear, cool waters of a pond. His strong shoulders and narrow hips were emphasized by his long legs stretching toward her. There was an aura of strength surrounding him, but his heart, which made him determined to help his cousin, was gentle. A faint smile curved his lips and shimmered in his remarkable grass-green eyes.

"What?" she whispered, unable to speak louder.

"It's not like Annie Wagler to acquiesce so fast. I guess I don't know you any better than I know my cousin, ain't so?"

Ready to say she'd be happy to tell him anything he wanted to know, she halted herself. How could she tell him she treasured moments like this when the two of them were alone and spoke of important matters? Of how she sensed a sweet intimacy that urged her to abolish the walls around her heart and allow her to tell him how important he'd become to her in the past year?

She couldn't. She'd come to the bakery this morning, resolved to do what she must to help him discover how Leanna would make him a *gut* wife. Why hadn't he taken her joking suggestion to invite Leanna to do chores with him instead of insisting he'd persuade Annie to like working in the barn? There had to be a way to get her sister and Caleb to spend some time together.

Lowering her eyes, she said, "I'll talk with Becky Sue, but you have to be part of the conversation, too."

"Won't that defeat the purpose of having you talk to her?"

She shook her head. "If I speak with her alone, she might reveal something I won't recognize as a clue to the truth because, other than Miriam, I don't know much about your family."

"That's sensible. We'll have to work out where and when."

"Let's think about it. If she thinks we're conspiring against her, she'll refuse to talk to us." She bent to collect the roller again. She stared at the wall in front of her as she asked, "Now that's settled, will you do me a favor?"

He didn't falter. "Sure. I owe you big-time. What can I do for you?"

Chapter Eight

Annie was taken aback by Caleb's question. She hadn't expected him to agree so quickly. She'd figured he would ask what the favor was first.

Or maybe she shouldn't be surprised. He was a man of integrity. His steady, fair way of listening to everyone had smoothed rough edges as a diverse group from several different districts and states had merged into one.

Now he'd agreed to do her a favor. Without a single quibble. All she had to do was ask.

But it wasn't easy.

The words weren't difficult. Words had never been a problem for her.

Yet she hesitated. Once she told him what she'd practiced for hours last night when she should have been sleeping, and he agreed to do her the favor, her heart would take a sharp blow. She couldn't put her own happiness above her sister's. Dear Leanna had been so sad for too long, pretending to accept the fact that the man she loved had married another without bothering to tell her.

Taking a deep breath, she said, "The Salem Volunteer Fire Department is having a mud sale, which is coming up."

"I know. In about three weeks." He gave her a cheeky grin, and her heart skidded for a moment before regaining its beat. "I don't want to brag, but it was my idea to have the auction to raise money as they do in Lancaster County."

"So you're going."

He glanced around the kitchen. Boxes had been shoved into any possible space to allow room to work. As if he'd spoken his thoughts aloud, she guessed he was wondering if he could afford to take the day of the mud sale off because there was so much to be done in order for the bakery to open its doors in May.

"I don't think I should miss what was my idea, ain't so?" he asked.

"Probably not."

"Are you planning to go?"

"*Ja.* I mean… I assume I'll stop by at least part of the day."

She was making a mess of this. It should be simple. Ask for what she wanted. He'd already said he'd agree without finding out what she wanted.

How hard could it be?

Harder than she'd guessed.

Taking a deep breath, she put the paint roller into its tray. She stood straight and faced him. "Will you give Leanna a ride with you to the mud sale?" The words burst out of her in a rush.

He looked surprised. "Why? I'd assumed your family would be going together. Didn't you say something about Leanna donating a quilt?"

"I did, and I know she'd like to be there when it's auctioned off. With my *grossmammi* taking longer and longer to get ready to go anywhere, we might not be able to get to the firehouse before her quilt is sold."

"You don't have to worry. The quilts won't be sold until around noon. We want the biggest crowd possible for the quilt auction and for lunch itself."

Annie didn't want to say she'd known that. Why was it difficult to do what should be easy? She desperately wanted to see her sister happy. *Just say it!*

Before she could, Caleb's brow knit with concern. "Is Inez failing fast?"

"She has *gut* days and not-so-*gut* ones," Annie hedged. Why hadn't she devised some other excuse to persuade Caleb? "I don't want to take the chance Leanna will miss seeing who buys the quilt she made. Will you pick her up that morning?"

Puzzlement pulled at his face. "*Ja*, if that's what you want in exchange for helping me with Becky Sue."

"It's not a trade-off." Her voice sounded distant in her ears. Almost unrecognizable. Were those calm tones hers? How could they be when her stomach roiled and her heart, threatening to tear apart the weak patches she'd put on it, hammered like a cloudburst on a metal roof? "I was going to ask you anyhow."

"I made it easier for you by asking you to help me first."

"*Ja*, you did." She prayed God would forgive her for that half-truth. Everything about setting up this day between her twin and Caleb was tough because each word she spoke might be the very one that turned his thoughts to her sister forever. It was what she wanted. All of her except her heart.

But you can be friends with him when he's your brother-in-law, she tried to remind herself, but it was to no avail.

Then she told her to stop being selfish. If there was a chance—any chance at all—her sister could set aside her long months of grief and be happy again, it was well worth doing a bit of damage to her own heart.

It was, wasn't it?

The house was quiet because everyone else was either in bed or in their rooms preparing for the night. Annie was alone in the kitchen, and she was using the time to make some cookies for everyone to enjoy the next day. She'd doubled the recipe, planning to take a few extra to the bakery to share with Caleb when they had their midday break. For the first time since she'd got home, she felt as if she could draw a full breath. Spending time with her twin while preparing supper had made her so uncomfortable she'd thought everyone would notice.

Nobody had because Joey had been fussy. The *boppli* now had two teeth trying to break through, and he was miserable. Even the hard teething biscuits Annie had made for him, using an old family recipe, had failed to give him any comfort. They'd passed the little boy from one set of Wagler arms to the next. Each time, he would stop whining and crying for a few minutes as he patted each of them on the face, put his nose to theirs and gurgled his *boppli* talk to them. He had a name of sorts for each of them. "Wa-wa" for Juanita, "Lee" for Leanna and "Na-nee" for Annie. For Kenny, he said, "Ken." That delighted her brother, and Kenny and Joey laughed each time the *kind* said it.

Grossmammi Inez had made a concoction from herbs, lemon and sugar to put on his swollen gums. Rocking him to sleep, she'd given him to his *mamm* to take upstairs along with the rest of the paste to lather on if Joey woke in the night.

Annie sat at the kitchen table while the cookies baked. She enjoyed the aroma of the rich chocolate chips in the cookies while she let the quiet slip over her like a warm shawl. She read the circle letter that had been delivered in the morning's mail. Her momentary sense of peace had vanished by the time she read the five letters enclosed with the one she'd sent the last time the letter had come to her. She was supposed to pull that one out, throw it away and put in a new letter before posting the whole packet again to her cousin in Central Pennsylvania.

And she tried. In between putting trays in the oven and ten minutes later taking out the finished cookies, she'd pulled out a sheet of clean paper. While the latest batch cooked, her pen hovered over the paper. Each of the letters spread out on her table mentioned the writers' curiosity about whether anything had happened between Leanna and Caleb. Somehow, each of her friends had read between the lines to discern Annie believed her twin and the settlement's founder were attracted to each other.

She had news she could share, but she hesitated. Writing the words that Caleb was escorting her twin to the upcoming mud sale would make it too real.

"But you want it to be real," she murmured.

"Talking to yourself can be a sign of losing your mind."

At *Grossmammi* Inez's jesting voice, Annie half turned in her chair, astonished because she'd thought her *grossmammi* had retired for the night. The old woman had her hair braided and hidden beneath a black kerchief. When *Grossmammi* Inez reached for one of the letters on the table, Annie wanted to snatch it from her hands. Instead she got up and took out a cookie sheet before putting the last one in to bake.

Scanning the letter she held, *Grossmammi* Inez sat

at the table. Her breathing seemed more strained than yesterday.

"Did you make an appointment with the *doktor*?" Annie asked as she came to the table.

"Ja." Inez gestured toward the calendar hanging by the refrigerator. "For the first week in May."

"He didn't have anything sooner?"

"You know the *doktors* are at the clinic in Salem only a couple of days a week."

Annie bit her lower lip before she asked if her *grossmammi* had let the office know how much difficulty she was having breathing. Why ask? She already knew *Grossmammi* Inez would never complain like that, not even to medical staff.

"Maybe," Annie said, "we should go to Glens Falls or Bennington to one of the hospitals so you can be seen by a *doktor* there."

"I'd need to have an appointment with my *doktor* here first before they would see me."

Unless you went to the emergency room. Annie didn't want to say that aloud, because the suggestion would distress her *grossmammi*.

Grossmammi Inez patted Annie's hand. "You worry too much, Annie. Don't forget what was written in the eighth chapter of Romans. *And we know that all things work together for good to them that love God, to them who are the called according to His purpose.* Have faith everything will turn out right."

"I have faith, but…"

"You like to help things move a bit faster?" Inez tapped the letter she held.

Annie gave her *grossmammi* an ironic smile and hoped her cheeks weren't flushing. "You see me clearly."

"Eyes looking through love have a way of being clear-sighted."

"I wish that were true."

Grossmammi Inez put down the letter and folded her arms on the table. "So it's true."

"What's true?"

"You're matchmaking for your sister."

Annie was surprised the older woman didn't make it a question. "I want her to be happy."

"We all do." Her *grossmammi* sighed, her uneven breath breaking into it. "Who have you decided is the best match for your twin?"

Annie's gaze slipped toward the cookies cooling on the counter, then to the letters in front of her. A mistake, she knew, the instant her *grossmammi*'s followed.

"It's Caleb Hartz, ain't so?" *Grossmammi* Inez wagged a finger at her. "Don't look at me in shock, *kinskind.* If you want to keep a secret, don't give yourself away by letting your eyes focus on these letters filled with such interesting questions about your twin sister and Caleb."

"I never could fool you, *Grossmammi.*"

"True." Inez clasped her hands together as if in prayer. "But why Caleb, Annie? If anyone had asked me, I'd have said you're the one who likes Caleb Hartz."

"I do like him. He's a *gut* man." Annie pushed back her chair and went to open the oven door before the final batch of cookies burned. "After what happened to Leanna with Gabriel, she deserves a *gut* man in her life."

"Be that as it may, you're leaving out one important detail. The heart wants what it wants. I think that was written by an *Englisch* poet."

"Emily Dickinson," Annie said as she used a spatula to put the new cookies next to the others on the aluminum foil. "You're quoting many different sources tonight, *Grossmammi*."

"I didn't know who wrote those words. I saw them on a plaque in a store one time, and they've stayed with me."

"And I saw it in a gift shop when I was looking for a birthday card for Juanita." Annie smiled, hoping the time was right to change the subject. "Who would have guessed shopping was educational?"

"Educational? What did you learn from the quote, Annie?"

"That my heart wants my sister's heart to know happiness again."

"You can't choose how your sister feels, Annie. She has decided to mourn for what she couldn't have. *Ja*, the heart may want what it wants, but we can't be ruled by our hearts. The *gut* Lord gave us brains so we might remember His love flows through us. To turn our backs on it is what brings unhappiness. Once your sister recalls God loves her, no matter what happens, she can regain her joy with life and with Him."

Annie wished she could have her *grossmammi*'s strong faith. Maybe then she'd know what she was supposed to do.

Grossmammi Inez sighed again. "But you've already put your plans into motion, ain't so?"

"*Ja*."

"I'll pray God is using you as His tool, Annie, and it's not your impatience guiding you. And I'll pray it'll turn out as it should."

"I will, too." Annie wondered if she'd ever meant three words more seriously in her whole life.

* * *

Lyndon Wagler was washing the barn floor when Caleb walked in after dawn the following week. Annie's big brother was whistling tunelessly in time with his sweeping motions as he sent the water spraying across the concrete. Rivers flowed from under the stainless steel tank toward the drain beneath the sink hooked to the far wall.

"Gute mariye," Caleb called.

Lifting his thumb off the sprayer control, Lyndon turned to face him. "I didn't expect to see you so early, Caleb. Figured you'd be milking at this hour, too."

"Just finished, so I thought I'd come and talk to you."

"Sounds important." Lyndon draped the end of the hose over the reel on the wall and bent to turn off the water. "Is it something with finalizing our *Ordnung*?"

"You're asking the wrong guy. You'd have to ask Eli."

Lyndon gave a snort. "Just because you aren't married and you couldn't have your name in the lot doesn't mean you're not involved any longer."

Caleb nodded. Everyone in the new settlement had had a voice—directly or indirectly—in the establishment of the rules under which they would live. That was the way a plain community was run.

"So what brings you over here before breakfast?"

"I wanted to let you know my plans before they went any further," he said.

"Plans? For the bakery?" Lyndon laughed. "Now *you* are talking to the wrong person. I can warm up soup and make toast, but that's the extent of my culinary skills."

"No, this has to do with the mud sale."

"Ah, looking for donations? Rhoda has been experimenting with some cheese she thought she might offer for the auction. We plan to be there to work. Anything else you need from us?"

"No, it's not about donations." Caleb launched into a very terse explanation of the favor Annie had asked of him. He finished with, "I wanted to let you know, Lyndon."

"So Annie asked you to take Leanna to the mud sale?" Lyndon pushed back his hat and scratched behind his left ear.

"*Ja.*"

"Interesting…"

When Lyndon didn't say anything else, Caleb waited. Lyndon Wagler resembled his twin sisters. He was much taller than they were, and what was left of his hair was reddish brown, but he was like them in other ways. Sometimes he was as talkative and forthright as Annie. At other times he could be as reticent as Leanna. It seemed he was going to be the latter in the wake of hearing about the favor Annie had asked of Caleb.

Lyndon lifted two metal milk containers, and walked toward the door at the end of the open space. Caleb picked up a full milk can and followed. He hadn't planned on helping with the milking here after completing his own less than fifteen minutes ago. He'd assumed Lyndon would be done as well, then he noticed Kenny wasn't in the barn. The boy must not have helped that morning. Caleb remembered mornings, as a boy, when he'd stayed in bed so late he'd barely made it to school before the teacher rang the bell.

Caleb set the milk can next to the dairy tank. "I didn't want you to get the wrong idea."

"That you're interested in courting my sister?" Lyndon shook his head. "No, I suppose I shouldn't get that idea."

"Gut." Caleb went to the door opening into the barnyard, then paused. "It has nothing to do with any member of your family. I'm not looking for a wife."

"Got it."

Only later, when he was on his way to talk to Eli about helping load the bench wagon in preparation for the next service, did Caleb realize Lyndon hadn't specified which of his sisters he believed Caleb was talking about. Not that it made any difference. Caleb wasn't going to get involved with either Wagler twin. He'd learned his lesson about risking his heart and his dreams.

The hard way.

Chapter Nine

"I like to wash dishes," Becky Sue said with a laugh as she set a casserole pan in the drainer. "But I hate to dry and put them away."

"Most girls feel the opposite." Annie lifted a plate already half-dry from the stack in the drainer. During the past week, she and Becky Sue had got into the habit of doing the breakfast dishes together while *Grossmammi* Inez and Becky Sue did the chore for dinner because it was only the two of them and Joey at home for the noon meal. Leanna and Juanita had taken over the task for supper. "They don't want to get their hands greasy or splatter water on their clothes."

"But the dish detergent makes my hands feel as soft as if I'd been rubbing them against a sheep."

"There's lanolin in detergent." Annie chuckled. "And in sheep's wool."

"Too bad it's not in goats' wool. Leanna would have the softest hands around. She loves taking care of those goats, ain't so?"

"*Ja.* Right now, she's letting the does she's been milking go dry because the kids will be born in about two to three months. How Joey will love seeing them play! They're as inquisitive as he is."

Becky Sue scrubbed a plate as she stared out the window. "You're assuming we'll be here in two to three months."

"You know you're welcome."

"I know." She flashed a smile at Annie before rinsing the plate. "But I'm not sure how long we should stay."

"You won't leave without letting me know where you're going, will you?"

The girl looked at her again, in what Annie judged to be honest astonishment this time. "Why would you want to know?"

"Because this whole family cares about you and Joey. We won't force you to stay, but if you decide to leave, we'll want to know where you're bound so we can be assured you'll be okay."

"I didn't realize that."

"Look around. You and Joey are part of our family."

"Which makes Caleb part of your family, too. That's inconvenient, ain't so?" She shot a sly, sideways glance at Annie.

Without hesitation, Annie replied, "We're all family here in Harmony Creek Hollow."

"That's not what I'm talking about, and you know it."

Annie smiled. She wasn't going to get into a discussion of her relationship with Caleb. The sooner the teen figured that out, the better it would be.

"We have a *wunderbaar* community here," Annie said. "Not only the *Leit*, but our *Englisch* neighbors."

"My family would never accept an *Englischer* in any sort of relationship." Becky Sue glanced at Annie and then away, but didn't add anything else.

Had Becky Sue let slip that Joey's *daed* was an *Englischer*?

Annie wanted to ask, but finished the dishes in silence. By the time she put the last ones away, Becky Sue had already left to spend time with her son. Was the offhand comment a clue to the truth the girl had been hiding?

The day was flashing by, and Caleb was beginning to believe the kitchen would be done in time. The refrigerator and the freezer had been hooked up that morning, and the quartz counters were being delivered the next day. The butcher block for the island had been fabricated by his neighbor and friend Jeremiah. That would be in by week's end. After that, his attention would be on the front room where the baked goods would be sold.

Digging his fingers into his lower back, he stretched and tried not to groan at his tired muscles as he looked across the room to where Annie was unpacking paper supplies and putting them in the storage closet. He hadn't been certain how many bags and boxes to buy, but he'd know more once he saw how many customers came and, more important, how many returned.

"I thought about what you said about customers seeing the back wall," he called across the kitchen.

"You did?" She set a handful of flattened white boxes on the lowest shelf and then straightened. Pressing one hand against her lower back in a motion that copied his, she faced him. Fatigue shadowed her eyes and dimmed her bright smile.

Guilt lashed at him. Was he insisting she work harder than she should? In addition to helping at the bakery, she had her chores at home and kept an eye on his cousin and the *boppli*. Though she hadn't said much, he knew she was worried about her *grossmammi*. At least he'd been able to ease her concern about her sister getting to the mud sale in time to see her quilt auctioned. However, it seemed there must be other ways he could have helped than offering her sister a ride to and home from the mud sale.

What if he was escorting Annie instead of her twin sister? His mind lingered there. He'd driven Annie to the bakery and home many times, but there would be something different about riding with her to the firehouse south of the village. And when he drove her home at the end of the long, exciting day...

Caleb halted the thought before it could take him where he shouldn't go. Not if he wanted to keep his dream moving forward. He was keeping the doubts planted by Verba out of his head, and he must be as vigilant about banishing thoughts of how *wunderbaar* it would be to slip his arm around Annie's shoulders as they rode through the late-winter twilight and...

Again he squashed the image in his mind. It wasn't easy when he was looking at her by the closet door, so he cut his eyes to the cupboards that soon would be filled with more supplies. He couldn't forget how relieved he'd been to set aside the burden of establishing the settlement. How much heavier were Annie's obligations? And she couldn't step away from her duties to her family.

No, it wasn't that she couldn't. She *wouldn't*.

Just as she'd keep working with him for as long as he needed her.

Lord, don't let me take her for granted again. Help guide me to show her I appreciate her efforts. But not by asking her to walk out with him when he couldn't offer her anything but friendship.

Discovering she was waiting with unusual patience for him to continue, Caleb said, "*Ja*, I've been thinking about the color for the wall."

"It should be bright."

"Bright? Why?"

Annie crossed the kitchen and stretched out her arms. She motioned for him to come stand beside her. When he did, hoping she didn't sense that his back was protesting again from long hours of work, she turned to face the front of the building. She tugged on his sleeves, so he copied her motion.

"See?" she asked. "If the color of the wall catches their attention, their eyes will be drawn right to the display in the cases. And once they see the goodies for sale, they won't be able to leave without buying something. Even a small order to sample your baking."

"What color do you suggest?"

"Yellow."

He gave her a wry grin. "You didn't hesitate on that."

"It's my favorite color. Reminds me of sunshine and daffodils and cake batter."

"Not chocolate cake batter?" he asked as he walked toward the door. Taking his hanging coat off the wall, he pulled it on, trying not to wince as he stretched.

"*Gut* to eat, but not a color I'd want on the wall." She smiled while she came toward the rear of the kitchen. For a moment, she turned and considered the room again. "If you don't like yellow, there are other nice colors like blue or green or purple that would grab customers' attention."

"You aren't planning on using them all, ain't so?"

"Like painting stripes?" she laughed. "Not if you want *me* to paint the wall. My skills aren't up to that task. However, we can paint some rectangles in different colors, so you can consider them and make your choice."

"Sounds like a plan. Let's go into Salem next week, and we can look at the color choices at the hardware store."

"You want me to go with you?"

He nodded, pleased to be the one to disconcert her for once. "I'm sure they have lots of colors. I could use your advice on which to pick."

"But what if you don't like what I do?"

"I'll let you know." He lifted her coat off its peg and held it out for her to slip her arms into it. "You aren't the only one who'll be working here. I'm going to be spending a lot of time in this kitchen, too, next winter when work on the farm is slower again. It'll help if I like the color on the walls."

"Okay. I'll go with you to the store." Several emotions scurried across her face, but she turned away to pull on her coat, preventing him from discerning what she was thinking.

Why was she making such a big deal out of an errand to get paint?

Why was he?

His gaze slid toward her as he reached for his hat. His fingers were awkward and groped for the peg while he found himself admiring the curve of her neck in the moment before she slid her bonnet into place, blocking his view. She and her sister were identical, but there was something unique about Annie Wagler. Something vital and vivacious, so alive that being near her seemed to bring life to parts of him he'd thought long dead: hope, as well as belief in the best in others and in himself.

Annie drew her shawl over her shoulders, and he looked away so she didn't catch him staring at her. That might lead her to believe he had time in his life for more than his work. He didn't.

Caleb closed up the bakery and locked the doors, wondering why he bothered. Nobody had tried to get inside since Becky Sue and Joey had taken shelter there. Each time he had someone come to work at the bakery, he had to make sure he was there to open up for them.

He went to get Dusty from the rickety barn owned by the bakery's neighbors. The old couple living next door wasn't using the space, so they'd accepted the offer he'd made last week to rent the barn from them. They also told him his horse could use the field connected to the barn, which would work well when the weather warmed.

After hitching his horse to the buggy, he climbed in along with Annie. He gave her one side of the thick wool blanket, and she tucked it in around herself. She had to shift to sit closer to him, but he didn't mind.

Be careful, he warned himself. *Keep everything between you business.*

She was his sister's friend. He'd already told her brother he considered the twins to be friends.

But he couldn't ignore the fact that far too often he found himself gazing in Annie's direction, losing track of time as he watched her graceful motions or when he listened to her latest idea for the bakery.

He was shaken out of his musings when Annie murmured, "Becky Sue said some things today you should know about."

"And you're telling me only now? Why?"

"Because I've been fighting the feeling I'm betraying her confidences by sharing them with anyone else."

"Did she ask you to keep what she said to yourself?"

"No, but if I want her to be open with me, I can't blab what she tells me."

He put his gloved hand on top of her thick mitten. "Annie, you aren't blabbing. You're confiding in her cousin who's worried about her."

"Don't try to befuddle me, Caleb Hartz!" She yanked her hand from beneath his and folded her arms in front of her. "I get enough of that from Becky Sue with her half answers."

"I wasn't trying to confuse you. I was trying to make you feel better about telling me what she said."

For a long minute, Annie didn't reply. "You're right," she said at last, and he wondered what she'd decided during her silent discussion with herself. "If she were my cousin, I'd want to know everything."

He listened while she shared what Becky Sue had let slip during their conversation. Asking Annie to repeat as much of the conversation as she could, he considered what his cousin had said and in what order.

"Something doesn't add up," he mused aloud when she finished.

"What?"

"I'm not sure, but something seems off."

"I think so, too."

He glanced at her and saw her relieved smile. "What do you think is off in her story?"

"If Joey's *daed* is an *Englischer* she met in Lancaster County, why did she come here? It seems unlikely to me she met an *Englisch* boy from Salem when she was in Pennsylvania." She raised her hands to halt his reply. "I know what you're going to say. *Englischers* travel farther than we do, but that's not why I'm finding her tale hard to believe. If the boy is here, why hasn't he come forward?"

"Maybe he doesn't want to admit to the truth. Or maybe he doesn't know she's here."

Annie sniffed her derision. "Everyone knows everything about everyone in Salem. Isn't that what you told me?"

"I did." He thought about the careful questions he'd asked at the fire department, wanting to get advice from his *Englisch* friends as well as his plain ones about what to do to help his cousin and her *boppli*. "And you're right. I would imagine everybody within twenty miles has heard about our discovery at the bakery. Maybe she was honest when she said it was a coincidence she ended up here."

"Coincidence is, I believe, often God's way of giving us a second chance to right a wrong we may not have realized we did to someone else. Or to ourselves."

He gave her a half smile. "It sounds as if you've given this a lot of thought."

"I have since Becky Sue showed up."

"So have I." *And since I asked you to work for me when I intended to ask Leanna instead.*

"Give her a chance to be honest with you. If you keep pressing, you'll back her into a corner. That will make her distrust you more."

He nodded, knowing her advice was sound. They had to try to follow it in the hope the girl would finally be forthcoming about what had driven her from her home.

Chapter Ten

Sunday morning dawned with a hint of warmth, a promise winter wouldn't last forever. Caleb drove his buggy into the busy yard in front of James Streicher's house. The blacksmith had moved to the community late last summer, and he'd already become an integral part of the district.

Handing his buggy over to Eli Troyer's nephew, Kyle, who would put Dusty with the rest of the horses in a nearby meadow, Caleb walked to where the other members of the *Leit* were gathered by the house's front door.

The women and the men began to divide into two groups as he walked toward them along a narrow path cut into the deep snowbanks. He turned to his left to join the other men, but froze as if the temperature had dropped fifty degrees.

Only his eyes moved as he stared in painful astonishment when Joey, who was in Lyndon's arms, held up chubby arms to Jeremiah, babbling in excitement. The *boppli* had never seen Jeremiah before, but was eager for the man to take him. He batted Jeremiah's face, as he did the Waglers', and gave a deep chortle that rumbled beneath the conversations around them.

So Joey wasn't going through a stage where he didn't like men. He'd been content with Lyndon holding him and gone eagerly to Jeremiah. Yet he screamed in terror when Caleb came near. Had something changed? Caleb wasn't going to test that before services, so he avoided getting too close to the men and the *kind*.

Through the service, as he joined others in singing the long hymns and listened to Eli's sermon and prayed, he couldn't keep the questions quiet. Why had the little boy had such an instantaneous hatred of him? What could Caleb do to ease the little boy's fears?

Lord, give me some idea.

Church Sundays were always among Annie's favorite days of the month. She could spend time with her friends and catch up on their lives. Before Miriam and Sarah had married, they had joined her and Leanna for outings, like going grocery shopping or attending a charity dinner at the firehouse or special events in the village. Their Harmony Creek Spinsters' Club hadn't done anything together since before their weddings last fall. Or, as they'd decided when they started the group, the Harmony Creek Spinsters' and Newlyweds' Club, agreeing to change the name when one of them married. At the time, none of them had plans to marry, but Miriam and Sarah had in the past year.

Annie hoped it would soon be Leanna's turn to take marriage vows. But how would it be possible when Caleb hadn't asked her sister to the mud sale as he'd promised to do a week ago?

"Do you see what I see?" asked Miriam as she came to stand by the door. Its window offered a view of the snowy driveway and the yard marked with footprints where the *kinder* had been chasing each other.

"What?" Annie asked.

"Your sister and my brother." Miriam chuckled. She pointed to the twosome, who were standing a few feet from the house. "I don't remember the last time I've seen the two of them talking to each other."

"They've been very busy with their work." Did her voice sound as strained to Miriam as it did to her?

Caleb and Leanna's conversation ended, and her sister rushed toward the house at the same time Caleb walked toward his buggy.

Miriam didn't wait until Leanna had taken off her bonnet before she asked, "So did he finally ask you to the mud sale?"

Annie was pierced by surprise. Why? Caleb talking to his sister and getting her advice on how to ask Leanna wasn't anything out of the ordinary. Her own brother had sought out her insight and Leanna's when he started walking out with Rhoda. They'd been no older than Becky Sue then, but he kept saying he wanted a female point of view.

"He did." Leanna kept her gaze on the floor as she lifted off her bonnet and put it on the table with the others. "He's being very kind because he knows how long it can take to get our family going in the morning."

"I'm glad you'll be there to see when your quilt comes up for bid," Annie said. And she was.

Yet, at the same time, she couldn't help the feeling she was sliding into a deep pit where not a hint of sunlight would ever reach. No, she wasn't going to let sorrow overwhelm her as it had Leanna. Rather, she was going to be grateful her sister might escape the darkness left in the wake of her heartbreak.

Half listening while her sister and Miriam talked about the mud sale, Annie was startled when she heard a hiss close to her left ear. She turned and saw Becky Sue crooking a finger toward her.

Annie excused herself, though Miriam and Leanna were so immersed in their conversation she wasn't sure they noticed her leaving, and walked to where Becky Sue stood near a closed door.

"Is it true?" the teen said.

"Is what true?" Annie wished—just once—Becky Sue would clarify what she was saying.

"Caleb is walking out with Leanna?"

"You know we don't talk about such things." Annie didn't like her stern tone any more than the girl did. Softening it, she said, "Caleb is giving Leanna a ride to the mud sale."

"And home?"

Annie shrugged. Would Caleb offer her twin a ride home, too? If none of the other Waglers got there, he would. However, at least Lyndon, who was also a volunteer firefighter, would be going and could bring her home.

"Are you okay with this?" Becky Sue persisted.

"It's nice of your cousin to be so thoughtful." She wasn't going to admit she'd set up the whole thing because she wasn't sure if Becky Sue would keep that to herself.

"I thought *you* liked him."

"I do. He's a nice man and a *gut* boss."

"You know that's not what I mean."

"I know what you mean, but I also know Caleb asked Leanna and I'm glad she's going to be there for the quilt auction."

The teen folded her arms over her chest and frowned. "He asked you to join him in doing chores in the barn."

"How do you know that?"

"I hear things." Becky Sue shrugged insolently. "Like everyone else does. Why haven't you accepted his invitation? Don't you like my cousin?"

"I like him. I don't like working in the barn."

Becky Sue glowered at her, then spun on her heel and stamped away.

Annie went in the opposite direction, avoiding where Miriam and Leanna were giggling together as if they were no older than Becky Sue. She paused to grab her coat, bonnet and mittens. Fresh air might help because the house suddenly felt as small as a *kind*'s shoebox.

The wind had risen again, and Annie ducked her head into it as she strode out into the cloud-darkened afternoon. Was another storm coming? She was beginning to doubt winter would ever end.

Snow clung to her boots, trying to halt her on every step, but she pushed forward until she bumped into someone. Raising her eyes, she nodded to her brother who was talking to some other men who were getting their buggies ready to leave. He started to ask a question, but she turned away before he could.

He didn't call after her but she heard assertive footsteps give chase. Looking over her shoulder, she saw Caleb behind her. She wanted to groan. He was the last person she wanted to talk to. What would she say to him when he let her know he'd done her the favor she'd asked for?

"Can I have a minute?" Caleb asked as he caught up with her.

"Ja." She'd be glad to give him more than a single minute, but he should focus on Leanna. *"Danki* for asking Leanna to go with you to the mud sale."

He waved that aside as if it didn't matter. She realized his face was drawn. What was wrong? It couldn't be because Leanna had agreed. If he hadn't wanted to ask her, he would have said as much to Annie. They were honest with each other...about most things.

"Joey let Jeremiah Stoltzfus hold him today before the service. He didn't make a peep." Caleb's words fell over one another in his hurry to speak them. "But he screams anytime I'm near him."

Her self-pity became sympathy for him. She didn't have any right to feel sorry for herself when events were unfolding as she'd arranged, but Caleb had been hurt over and over by the *boppli*'s response.

"It's impossible to know what's going on in a *boppli*'s head," she said, putting a solacing hand on his sleeve and trying to ignore the strong muscles beneath the layers of wool and cotton. "It may not have anything to do with what you've been doing. Think about how Becky Sue is so tense around you. Maybe Joey thinks she's frightened of you, so he is, too. A one-year-old isn't going to understand why his *mamm* feels as she does."

"I'd like to believe you're right, but it's clear Joey hates me."

"A *boppli* doesn't hate anyone or anything. He's scared for some reason."

"*Danki* for trying to make me feel better, but you're using different words to say the same thing."

"Stop it!"

Annie's sharp words jerked Caleb out of his morass of shame. He stared at her, wondering why he was startled she wasn't reacting as he'd expected. She seldom did.

Her voice softened. "I know it bothers you, Caleb, that Joey cries, but he's a *boppli*. Like I said, none of us can guess what goes on in his head. He's a loving *kind*, want-

ing to touch us whenever we hold him. He'll warm up
to you when he sees you want to take care of him, too."

"I'd like to think—"

A sharp ring cut through the gray afternoon as his
pocket vibrated against his leg. The sound and the sensation repeated before he could move. Maybe everyone
didn't whirl to stare at him, but it sure felt that way.
Fishing the cell phone out of his pocket, he strode away
from Annie and the men gathered closer to the house.
He tapped the phone screen the way he'd been shown
and held it to his ear.

Nothing.

He'd missed the call.

Maybe it hadn't been important.

He looked at the screen, and his gut tightened as he
recognized the number. It belonged to the phone shack
that Becky Sue's family used!

He pushed another button to call back. He grimaced
when he heard a busy signal. Giving himself to the count of
twenty, he tried again with the same result. He waited another full minute—which felt like an eternity—and made
another attempt. This time, he got the same answering
machine he had before. Leaving a message to call him as
soon as possible, he ended the call.

Walking to where Annie stood, he glowered at the
phone. Why hadn't Becky Sue's family waited long
enough for him to call back? It didn't make sense. He
tightened his hold around the slender phone. It was almost as if they'd done their duty by calling and felt it
wasn't necessary to do anything else.

But didn't they want to know where their daughter and *kins-kind* were? Weren't they worried about
whether they were safe and had a place to sleep and
food to eat?

He tried to remember what message he'd left. It had been bare-bones facts that the two had been found and Caleb would make sure they were okay until Becky Sue's family sent instructions about whether they wanted him to bring her home or they wanted to come to Harmony Creek Hollow for a reunion with the runaway teen and her *boppli*. But if they'd taken time to make arrangements, why hadn't they waited for him to call and find out what they were?

"Was that Becky Sue's parents?" Annie asked.

"Ja."

"Are they coming here?"

He lifted one shoulder in a half-hearted response. "I don't know. I didn't answer the call in time, and when I called back, I didn't get an answer."

She put consoling fingers on his arm as she had before, and he felt his frustration melt away beneath her warm touch. How did Annie manage to do that with a simple brush of her fingertips on his sleeve?

"The important thing is they called," she said.

"Ja." He looked at the phone as he added, "When I tried calling them back, the line was busy."

"A *gut* sign someone is in the phone shack."

How did she always see the best side of every circumstance? While he looked for problems so he could avoid them, she seemed to believe everything would be fine if she moved ahead.

"But then the answering machine picked up."

Her eyes widened, and he looked away before he lost himself in their enticing depths.

"That's strange," she said. "I would have guessed that they'd hang around long enough to wait for you to call."

"I thought so, too. But—"

Again he was interrupted by a sound from the phone. This time it was a chirping noise.

Caleb looked at the screen to see an announcement that there was a voice mail. Hoping he was remembering the correct way to retrieve it, because it'd been a few weeks since his friend had showed him how to use the various utilities on the cell phone, he tapped the screen before holding the device to his ear. He listened, then lowered it, shocked at what he'd heard. Pushing the buttons again, he held it to his other ear, hoping that what he thought he'd heard was a mistake.

It wasn't.

"Was that a message from Becky Sue's *mamm* or *daed*?" Annie asked.

Without a word, he handed her the phone. He motioned for her to activate the voice mail, and she followed his silent instructions.

He knew the moment she heard the words that had sent disgust rocketing through him. Her face flushed and tears filled her eyes as she looked at where Becky Sue was emerging from the house surrounded by the Waglers.

The words spoken in a man's clipped tones were seared into Caleb's brain. "You've got Becky Sue. Keep her. We don't want her or her *boppli* here."

Chapter Eleven

Annie frowned at the windows in the bakery's front room. Her fingers itched to dip a cloth into hot, soapy water so she could begin to wash the layers of grime from the glass. As soon as the cold weather broke, she intended to give the windows in both rooms a *gut* cleaning. She imagined how sunshine would glint off the polished glass cases where cakes and pies and cookies and other sweets would be displayed.

Each day, Caleb brought in a product he wanted to sell at the bakery and asked her opinion. She'd sampled whoopie pies as well as cookies and cake and cinnamon rolls. Every one had been delicious, a sure sign that the bakery would be a success.

For the past week, she and Caleb had been working on the main room of the shop. He'd repaired windows and started nailing down the loose floorboards, replacing some that would no longer fit into place. She suspected he was easing his frustration with Becky Sue's parents by slamming the hammer into the boards. Several times a day, he tried calling their number and he left dozens of messages.

None were returned.

How could parents wash their hands of their *kind* and *kins-kind* like that? Annie couldn't come up with an answer for that puzzling question.

She felt her own frustration fall from her shoulders when she drew in a deep breath. The astonishing aroma of chocolate chip cookies would, she decided, never grow old. She was eager to sample Caleb's recipe, which added a touch of maple syrup to the dough. He was baking them today to check the temperature in the double ovens and make sure he wouldn't burn products when he was ready to open the doors in a few weeks.

At the happy chirp of the timer, she went into the kitchen and grabbed a pot holder and the waiting trays of cookie dough he'd prepared before he went out to pick up some debris that had blown against the building during the previous night's storm. She opened the wide door on the ovens, which had more controls than she'd imagined any appliance could. Switching the two trays and resetting the timer, she let the enticing scent of baking cookies swirl around her.

She slid the cookies off the tray and put another batch in their places, so they could go in when the others were done. Feeling like a naughty child, she picked up a warm cookie. She took a bite and grinned. The rich flavor of maple syrup was subtle but enhanced the luxurious chocolate and pecan bits mixed into the dough.

Golden maple syrup…

Annie glanced at the kitchen wall that remained a boring white. The plans to go to the hardware store to get paint had been pushed aside day after day while they finished tasks inside the building. Supplies had arrived and had to be unpacked. A couple of roof slats had been cracked by an ice dam, so Caleb had spent a day repairing the damage where water seeping past the broken slats had turned a section of the ceiling brown.

She looked at the calendar where Caleb crossed off each day. They had five weeks before opening day. Would they make it?

The door opened and Annie started to greet Caleb. She choked on the cookie when Leanna walked in.

"What are you doing here in the middle of the afternoon?" Annie asked after taking a gulp of water to wash down the crumbs. "Isn't today your day to work at Mrs. Beattie's house?"

Leanna untied her bonnet. "She asked me to skip this week because her daughter's visiting. I thought I'd stop by and see what's been keeping you so busy." She hung her bonnet by the door. Scanning the space, she whistled. "This is fancier than I expected."

Annie began to explain how Caleb had bought the appliances and extra cabinets from Mr. Summerhays. When her twin frowned, Annie realized how defensive she sounded.

"It was a blessing that the appliances were available," Annie said as she hurried to finish.

"I guess it would have been *dumm* not to take advantage of such an opportunity, ain't so?" Leanna stood in the center of the room so she could take in every inch of it. "How many bakers is he planning to hire?"

"I don't know."

"He can't intend to use all this by himself."

"I told him, though he hired me to run the cash register and deal with customers, I'd be willing to help with baking." Annie gave a careless shrug. "Of course, it's going to depend on how many customers he gets and what products they buy."

Leanna began to count on her fingers. "Whoopie

pies, all sorts of cookies, fresh bread and biscuits, cakes and, of course, pies. Especially shoofly pie. That seems to be everyone's favorite plain treat."

"*Komm*, and I'll show you the front room where the customers will shop. We're still working on it."

As she led the way into the other space, Annie held her breath. Would Leanna see past the work still to be done? Annie no longer saw the stained walls or how the glass display cases needed their doors set into place. Instead she imagined the walls painted a soft shade, and tables and chairs on one side filled with happy people and others gazing at a chalkboard listing products along with their prices as more eager customers stood in a long line winding out the door.

"I didn't think it'd be this big," Leanna said. "The counter and display case don't take up much room."

"I suggested that Caleb put some tables in for customers."

"That would fill up the empty space, ain't so? Is he going to do it?"

"He's deciding."

"What's to decide? If people come in and the place looks empty, they'll think there's something wrong and go away."

"He'll make up his mind when it's the proper time," Annie said, though she agreed with her sister.

"I hope he doesn't wait too long. Isn't he opening at the beginning of May?"

"*Ja.*" Why was she trying to justify Caleb's decisions to Leanna? He was her boss, and the choices he made for the bakery were his and his alone. "Want a cookie?"

"Sounds *gut*."

Leading her twin back into the kitchen, Annie went to the ovens a second before the timer beeped. She exchanged the trays again, then motioned for her sister to select a cookie or two.

The door opened, and the icy wind swirled through the kitchen, making the May opening seem a long, long time off. Annie wrapped her arms around herself, but the motion couldn't stave off the cold.

Caleb knocked snow off his boots before he stepped into the kitchen. Above his scarf, his eyes crinkled with a smile. He yanked off the scarf, letting it fall over one shoulder.

"Leanna! What brings you here today?" Caleb's smile broadened as he walked past Annie, paying her no more attention than if she'd vanished.

Her twin brightened as she flung out her hands. "My curiosity got the better of me, and I couldn't wait for the bakery to open to see what has kept you and Annie so busy here."

He began to list the tasks they'd done as if her words hadn't affected him. A bright red flush rising from his shirt told Annie otherwise. He was flustered by her sister's comments.

When he began to repeat Annie's tour, Leanna shot her a glance warning not to interfere. Or was it meant to tell Annie to find something else to do so her twin could spend time alone with Caleb?

Annie hated how her happiness had vanished. She should be thrilled that her twin had come to the bakery to get a preview of the shop, but being ignored stung. Or was she being too sensitive because Caleb smiled at her when he asked her what she thought of his recipe for the chocolate chip cookies?

"They're delicious, Caleb. Once people taste them, they're going to fly off the shelves. If…" Her voice trailed away when she realized he wasn't listening to her as he strode with Leanna into the front of the shop.

Glancing at the timer and seeing she had a couple of minutes before the cookies were done, she rushed after them. Word had spread that Leanna was riding to the mud sale with Caleb. Thanks to Becky Sue, Annie was sure, but people would look at Leanna and Caleb differently if it was assumed they were walking out together. Though they were adults, long past teens on their *rumspringas*, there must be no question of impropriety.

Becoming a chaperone for Caleb and Leanna was something she hadn't considered, and she wondered if she'd ever been more uncomfortable than she was when she joined them in the front room. They were busy talking, Caleb repeating much of what Annie had already told her twin and Leanna acting as if she was hearing it for the first time.

Did they even notice she was there?

She flinched when she heard Caleb say her name, then realized he remained focused on her sister.

"Annie mentioned," he said as he smiled at Leanna, "that you might want to display some of your small quilts here. I'm hoping we'll get plenty of *Englisch* tourists on their journeys to and from Vermont."

"And *Englischers* love small quilts they can hang in their homes," Annie hurried to add so she couldn't be accused of sneaking into their conversation. "The colors would be pretty in the shop, as well."

Leanna looked at the graying floorboards. "That's true." Turning to Caleb, she said, "I've got some pieces that I could bring in when you're ready to open. Wall hangings and pot holders and other little items like that. If anyone is interested in any of them, then I can make more to replace the ones that sell."

"What about a full-size quilt?" Annie asked. "One to put on the wall behind the tables."

Caleb frowned. "I haven't made up my mind about having tables."

"I know, but I thought—"

"I said I'd think about it, and that's what I'm doing."

She opened her mouth to protest, but closed it when Leanna laid gentle fingers on her arm. How many times had her twin used the same motion to warn her to be silent before she spoke and got herself into trouble?

Mumbling some half-formed excuse, Annie went into the kitchen to start cleaning the baking pans and other dishes. She scraped off stuck-down pieces of cookie from the sheets before putting them in the dishwasher along with the mixing bowls. As she started the machine she'd learned to use, she heard laughter from the other room.

She felt more alone than she had in her whole life, because she had to envision her life without Leanna being a big part of it. But worse was knowing everything was about to change between her and Caleb, too. She should have been beside herself with joy, but all she could feel was sadness and loss.

Caleb drove the last—or he hoped it was the last—nail into the floorboard closest to the front door. Sitting on his heels, he looked along the floor. It wasn't even near the trap door. Though he didn't want his customers to trip, he'd decided against nailing that shut until he decided if he'd have to use the storage space under it. He'd seen low-pile carpet at the hardware store, but it would show wear quickly. Until he had enough money to pay for several truckloads of gravel to cover the muddy parking lot, the carpet would be filthy within an hour of his opening the door each morning. This old floor would have to do until he could find the time and the money to put in a new one.

Pushing himself to his feet, he picked up the box of nails and his hammer. He carried them into the kitchen, where Annie was emptying the dishwasher. Because the state health inspector would require such a machine in a bakery kitchen, Caleb had had it installed. It was loud and made clouds of steam, but it made sure the dishes and utensils were sanitized before their next use.

"How's it going?" he asked when Annie didn't greet him.

She'd been strangely quiet since her sister left. He hoped they hadn't had an argument. He'd never seen them quarrel, but siblings had differences of opinions at times. Certainly he and Miriam had when they were growing up.

"The dishes are clean," she replied, "and I put the cookies in a sealed container so they won't go stale soon."

"Why don't you take them home? Leanna gave them her approval, and I'd like to hear what the rest of your family thinks."

"Okay."

What was going on? They might as well have been strangers for how little she was talking to him. If the problem was between her and her sister, he'd be wise not to get in the middle of it. Anytime Annie had had a problem with him, she hadn't been averse to letting him know right away.

"Caleb?" she called as he turned to put his tools away.

"Ja?"

"As we're going to use the dishwasher regularly, the

detergent should be stored under the sink. Where did you put it?"

"Under the sink."

"It's not there now."

"No?" Baffled, he asked, "What did you use to clean those dishes?"

"There was a small cup with detergent in it. That's empty. Where else could the big container be?"

"I don't know. Maybe in the storage closet," he replied, though he wondered how the plastic container, which he remembered placing under the sink, had moved.

He didn't need enigmas. He must concentrate on the dozens of tasks waiting for him. Catching a flash of motion out the window, he reminded himself that if he didn't order the blinds they wouldn't be ready for the bakery's opening. The front of the building faced west, and the afternoon sun would be pitiless on his customers and his products.

Annie went to the closet, opened the door and walked inside, holding out one hand to keep the door from slamming shut. A moment later, she shouted from the closet. "I see the detergent, but it's up too high for me to reach."

Knowing that there wasn't enough space for the step stool in the closet that was stacked high with unpacked boxes, he put down the hammer and crossed the kitchen. He motioned for her to move so they could exchange places.

She stepped into the kitchen, and he squeezed into the cramped space. He shifted a couple of the heavy cases into the kitchen before he could bump into them and knock them over. Nothing was breakable in them, because they contained napkins and other paper supplies, but he wanted to keep the cardboard boxes from breaking and spewing paper everywhere.

He ran his fingers along the topmost shelf, but didn't find the plastic bucket. When the cleaning supplies had been delivered, he'd put it against the right wall within easy reach for him. But then he'd moved it under the sink.

"Can you guide me to where it is?" he asked. "I can't see it from where I'm standing."

She slipped into the closet, letting the door close behind her. She pointed up. Her fingers were a bare inch from his nose, and she edged her arm away.

He realized she couldn't move more because there wasn't much space between him and the filled shelves and crates. Since he'd been depending on her to get supplies out of the cramped closet, he hadn't guessed how difficult it was to retrieve anything. He should build more storage space, but that would cut into the kitchen area. Something else to put on his to-consider list once the bakery was open and he had a better idea of how many customers would be stopping by each day.

"To your left," Annie directed.

"Left? It should be on the right."

"Maybe it should be, but it's on the left side. Second box in. A bit farther to your left," she added when he ran his fingers along the shelf again. "A little bit farther. There!"

He rose on tiptoe and closed his fingers around what he hoped was the correct container. "This one?"

"*Ja.* I think so. Your head is blocking my view."

"Sorry. I don't think it's removable."

When she laughed, he was delighted that his weak joke had shattered her coolness in the wake of her sister's visit. The sound made his heart hitch and then beat faster.

As he pulled the container off the shelf and lowered it between his chest and the shelves, he heard her turn the doorknob so she could get out of his way.

"Anything else you need?" he asked when she didn't open the door.

"The key."

"What?"

Annie tried the doorknob again. It refused to turn. She tried to jiggle the door, wondering if something had got stuck in the latch.

"What's going on?" Caleb asked as he eased away from the shelves. When he bumped into her, he repeated the question.

"The door is locked."

"What do you mean?"

She rolled her eyes. "I mean it's locked. The door won't open."

"Let me try."

Wanting to tell him she doubted he'd have different results, she edged aside, giving him room. She tried to make herself small so he could reach past her to grab the doorknob.

His bare forearm beneath his rolled-up sleeve stretched past her, touching hers. Her skin prickled where his brushed against her. His muted, quick intake of breath told her she wasn't the only one aware of the enticing sensation. She jerked her arm away, holding it close to her like a shield.

He didn't look at her as he yanked on the doorknob. It didn't move.

"Here." He handed her the bucket of dishwasher detergent. "Can you move back?"

"I don't think so."

Glancing everywhere but at her, he startled her as he grasped her by the waist. A squeak of surprise burst from her when he lifted her and sat her on one of the boxes as if she were no older than Joey.

"This might give us a bit more room," he said.

"Okay." Her voice shook with the tempest of emotions roiling through her like a summer storm.

As he turned to try the door again, Annie took a steadying breath. What was wrong with her? She'd witnessed him spending time with her sister and lavishing attention on Leanna. Anyone seeing them together would have assumed they were a couple. If all went as Annie planned, Caleb and Leanna soon would be walking out together.

She was saved from having to imagine a future with Caleb as her sister's husband when he slapped the door with his palm. It didn't open.

"How could it be locked?" he asked.

"I don't know."

He looked over his shoulder at her and gave her a half grin. "I didn't expect you did. That was my frustration talking. But the door shouldn't be able to lock on its own."

"True, and we've got to figure a way to get out of here." She rested her hands on her apron that was spotted with water from her work in the kitchen.

"If you don't show up for supper, someone will come here to look for you, ain't so?"

"I'm not worried about that. I'm worried about the kettle on the stove. I was going to make us some tea."

"You left it on?"

As if answer to his question, the whistle from the kettle announced the water was boiling.

When Caleb whirled to face her, she gave him a

scowl to match his. "I wasn't planning to take more than a couple of seconds to get the detergent. I didn't think I needed to take the kettle off."

"Of course not." He sighed and rubbed his eyes. "We've got to get out."

"The kettle is pretty full, so it shouldn't boil dry for a while."

"Fifteen minutes?"

She nodded. "Do you have that cell phone you borrowed?"

"No. I returned it a couple of days ago."

"How about that pager thing you wear?"

He looked at his waist and the small device the volunteer firefighters wore. "It lets us know where there's an emergency. It doesn't call out."

"Pounding on the door won't get us anywhere."

He sighed as he looked around the cramped space that was lit by the faint light coming around the door. "If I had my tools, I could pop the pins out of the hinges and remove the door."

"But they're outside in the kitchen."

"Ja."

The kettle's whistle went up in pitch as if it sensed the urgency of the situation.

He eased past her knees, the momentary contact of his chest against them propelling the powerful awareness through her again. With a mumbled apology, he faced the outer wall. He pushed on one side of what once had been the sliding door, but it was securely nailed in place.

The kettle continued singing out its warning.

They had to get out.

"It's going to be okay," Caleb said.

Annie stared at her hands, knowing her distress must

have been visible on her face. "I should have taken the kettle off when I came to get the detergent."

"You couldn't have known, Annie. If you want to blame anyone, blame me for not checking the door's lock."

She shuddered when the kettle's whistle seemed to reach a higher pitch. Did that mean the water was boiling away faster?

"I'm sorry, Caleb," she whispered.

His hand under her chin tilted her face up so she couldn't avoid looking at him as he stood right in front of her. Whatever he'd intended to say was lost as his gaze locked with hers. Unlike ever before, they were on the same level, and she saw silvery flecks in his vivid green eyes.

Her breath caught when his fingers uncurled along her cheek, cupping it. All thought vanished but of how sweet his touch was. His eyes sought something in hers. What? She didn't know, but she was willing to let him discover every secret in her heart…even how much she longed for him to kiss her. She slanted toward him, not closing her eyes because she didn't want to break the connection between them.

Suddenly he pushed forward into her. His hands caught her by the waist, steadying her so she didn't tumble off the box. She grabbed his shoulders before her chin slammed into his.

Annie gasped as she looked past him and saw his cousin standing in the doorway. Becky Sue pushing the door open must have been what had shoved Caleb into her.

"What are you two doing in the closet?" the girl asked with a giggle.

Realizing it must look as if she and Caleb were embracing, Annie lifted her hands away from his shoulders. He stepped back, and she jumped off the box, straightening her clothing that had got mussed beneath her. Without a word to either of them, she rushed to the stove and turned off the burner. She took the kettle off it, wincing as the heat scorched her hand.

Caleb put the detergent container by the sink before facing his cousin and asking, "Did you lock the door, Becky Sue?"

"Why would I do anything like that?" She motioned toward where Annie was cradling her burnt hand in the other one. "I was out, so I stopped by to see what you two were up to. I heard the kettle screeching, then heard noise from the closet. I opened the door, and there you were." Her smile became sly. "Looking very comfortable together."

Shocked by her insinuation and worried that Becky Sue would carry the tale to Leanna and others, Annie said, "Comfortable was the last thing we were. Hearing the kettle, knowing the water was boiling away and the bakery could go up in flames doesn't make anyone *comfortable*."

The girl gave them a flippant shrug and then a wave before she left. As the door closed behind Becky Sue, Annie frowned. The teenager had said she was "out," but not where she'd been or where she was going or why. It was suspicious.

Saying the same to Caleb, Annie added, "She must have locked us in."

"I agree. I wish I had some idea why. My thought when I saw her on the other side of the door was she'd changed her mind about planning to use the time to slip away from Harmony Creek Hollow while we were shut in the closet."

"I've given up trying to figure out what she's thinking."

"I should, too." He gave Annie a smile that sent delight swirling through her middle again. "How about that cup of tea you had planned?"

There was so much Annie wanted to say about how his touch had thrilled her. So much she wanted to ask about whether or not he'd shared her feelings. Would he have kissed her if the door had remained shut a moment longer?

It was better, she told herself as she went to find tea bags, that she didn't know. Better for her matchmaking plans for her twin. Better for Caleb, who wouldn't be torn between them. Better for everything…except her aching heart.

Chapter Twelve

As Caleb's buggy reached the pair of stoplights at the very heart of the village, where Broadway and Main Street intersected, the light snow changed into a heavy fall. Caleb stopped for the red light. Going in the other direction, cars had slowed to a crawl, their windshield wipers fighting against the snow piling up on the glass. A couple of shopkeepers were already outside brushing snow off the stone steps leading up to their front doors. *Kinder* rushed along the sidewalk, hunched into their coats. Not even youngsters were excited any longer by snow after the hard winter.

"I remember when snow was fun and not something that gets in the way," Caleb said as he switched on the wiper on the front of his buggy.

"I still think snow is fun." Annie opened her door and ran her hand over the window to knock off the snow, so he could see any oncoming traffic to the left.

Thanking her, because they must take extra care that a car would be able to stop on the snow-covered road, he chuckled. "Why am I not surprised? You somehow always find something positive."

"Isn't that better than the alternative? Finding something depressing about every situation?"

"Are you saying I do that?"

She laughed, "No, but if the boot fits…"

"It doesn't fit well. Or, at least, I hope it doesn't."

When she chuckled again, he relaxed as he hadn't been able to since he'd picked her up at her house. She'd been as serious and quiet this morning as she'd been yesterday afternoon before they somehow got themselves locked into the closet…or were shut in with Becky Sue's help. It hadn't helped that Joey had launched into shrieks the moment Caleb walked into the Waglers' house. Annie had rushed him out so the others could calm the *boppli*, who wanted nothing to do with him.

Was he the only one the *boppli* reacted to like that? Annie, for once, had no suggestions other than to be patient. It was *gut* advice, but hard to follow when Caleb wanted to put the *kind* at ease.

Caleb turned the buggy north along Main Street toward the hardware store on the right side of the street. He'd hoped the snow would hold off until they got home from the long-postponed trip to get paint. Clouds covering the tops of the mountains had descended into the valley, bringing the storm with them. Already plowed snow blocked the wide parking lane beside the sidewalk, narrowing it until there was room for only a single car instead of the usual two.

He saw Annie's surprise and realized she'd expected him to leave the buggy and horse by the hitching rail near the library.

Drawing in the reins to stop them closer to the hardware store, he said, "As fast as it's snowing, the plows will be out soon. Dusty will be safer here between cars than in the open where the spraying snow could strike him."

"I didn't think about that." She chuckled. "I thought that—for the first time ever—you were breaking the rules."

"I am. The village leaders have asked us to park the horses by the library or at the hitching rail in front of the grocery store."

"No, you're not breaking the rules. You're protecting Dusty."

"Isn't that the same thing?"

When he looked at her as the buggy rolled to a stop, he saw she was grinning and shaking her head. "Maybe for others. But for you, Caleb, breaking such rules is a big deal."

He decided the best answer was to laugh, so he did. As he got out and scaled the snowbank beside the buggy, he wondered what else she could discern about him. No other woman—or any man, to be truthful—had tried to look beyond the obvious to pick out the truth he kept close to his heart. Yet Annie had been able to do that almost from the moment they'd met. He recalled the questions she'd asked him when he came to talk to her family about the settlement he envisioned. Those questions had been insightful and demanded he be honest at the same time.

As he stepped onto the sidewalk that was littered with snow, he realized her questions made him lower the barriers he kept up between the world and himself. And between his head and his heart, as if he didn't trust them to work together.

"Did you forget something?" Annie called as she climbed the steps to the hardware store's front door.

Shaking his head, and sending snow flying from the brim of his hat, Caleb hurried to catch up with her. He had to keep focused on making his dreams come true instead of daydreaming about Annie.

She led the way to where cans of paint flanked sample cards. The lighting in the hardware store wasn't strong, and shadows covered most of the displays of tools and equipment lining every wall. The long wooden counter at the rear of the store was deserted, but he knew Tuck, who owned the hardware store, would pop out when they were ready to buy something.

"What do you think?" she asked.

He stared at the array of colors. "I don't know where to begin."

She reached out and pulled a card with several shades of yellow on it. She tapped the middle one. "There's the color I was envisioning. You might want to look at it over by the window to see it better." She handed it to him.

For the very shortest possible moment, their fingertips touched. A spark as hot as if he'd grabbed a welding torch seared him. A buzzing sensation lingered as he fought not to fumble taking the card. His other hand rose toward her face, partially concealed by her black bonnet. He lowered it before he could give in to his longing to touch her as he had in the closet yesterday.

"You like this yellow?" he managed to ask, though his brain was urging him to step closer to her.

"It's bright and cheerful." She drew out another card. "Then there's this blue. It may go better with the wood on your display cases."

How could she sound so calm? He was sure he'd seen her pull back in shock, too. Then he noticed she was speaking at a rapid clip as she pulled out several more cards and outlined the pros and cons of each color. She wasn't as serene as she was trying to appear. Could she be drawn to him?

That was silly.

As she talked about painting sample patches on the wall and deciding which one was best after viewing several, he nodded, half listening. If Annie was interested in being more than his friend and employee, why had she asked him to take her sister to the mud sale instead of her? He must be missing something.

He wished he knew what.

Annie stepped back, being careful not to bump into the paint sample containers she'd put on the kitchen floor. Five large rectangles gleamed on the wall. Yellow, blue, green, tan and gray. She couldn't wait for them to dry so Caleb could choose which one he liked best.

She bent to screw on the gray sample's lid. She straightened with a gasp when the door opened, nearly hitting the container holding the yellow sample. Grabbing it, she jumped out of the way as Caleb rushed into the bakery.

She took one look at his face and asked, "What's wrong?"

"Becky Sue has disappeared!"

Staring at him, hoping she'd heard him wrong, she repeated, "Disappeared? Has she run away again?"

"It seems so." Pushing back his black hat that drooped toward his eyes with the melting snow on its brim, he said, "Miriam alerted me. Becky Sue stormed out when my sister insisted she help with some chores. Did she come here?"

"No." Annie sighed. At the Waglers' house, the tug-of-war between *Grossmammi* Inez and the girl had been growing more heated. She hadn't guessed that Becky Sue was being as obstinate with Miriam. "Did she go home…to our house?"

"No."

"Maybe she went into town."

"It would take her an hour on foot to go to Salem. She'd be foolish to make such a trip on a stormy day. Drivers wouldn't see her until they were almost upon her."

"Vanishing like this is already foolish." She whirled as the timer beeped. Rushing to the stove, she opened the door and pulled out the cookies. She didn't set the other tray inside to bake.

As she used the spatula to push the cookies onto the aluminum foil, she watched Caleb open the storage closet and look inside. He didn't doubt her assertion, she knew, but he had to see for himself that his cousin hadn't taken advantage of Annie's focus on her baking to slip past her.

"Do you think this has anything to do with where she was the other day when we got locked in the closet? She said she was out, but didn't explain where she was going." She pulled off the pot holder and set it on the table beside the cookies.

He drew in a deep breath through clamped lips and then shook his head as he walked into the front room. "I don't have the slightest idea what that girl will do next."

"What about Joey?"

He bent and opened the trap door in the floor. Closing it, he answered, "She didn't take him."

Annie watched him stamp into the kitchen. "I don't believe Becky Sue has run away. She wouldn't leave him behind. Not when…"

He spun to face her. "Not when he's terrified of me."

"Caleb, this isn't the time for discussing the whims of a one-year-old. If your cousin has gone missing, something could be very wrong."

"Don't you think I know that?" He paced the kitchen, his boots striking the concrete floor as if he intended to drive his feet right through it. "Do you know who her friends are? Beyond our families, I mean."

"I don't think she has made any yet."

"There must be some clue to where she is."

Annie planted herself in front of him. When he started to go around her, she grasped his sleeves and forced him to halt before he dragged her off her feet. "Calm down, Caleb. We've got to think about this rationally."

"Even when she's not being logical?"

"It's more important *we* think clearly." She looked at the falling snow. "We need help. We might not be able to find her on our own."

The wild light dimmed in his eyes as he nodded. "*Danki*, Annie, for your *gut* sense." He shifted his arms so he could grip hers. "Wait here while I get help."

"No!" She reached for her coat.

"It's so cold, Annie, and I don't have my regular buggy."

"Where's your…?" She answered her own question. "Becky Sue took it, ain't so?"

"It's gone. She's gone. You do the math." He sighed. "You'd be better off staying inside."

"I'm going to get cold when I walk home, so what does it matter if I get cold now? We have to find Becky Sue before something happens to her."

He was torn. She could see that. He didn't want to miss a minute of them working on the bakery, but he was worried sick about his young cousin.

At last, he nodded and motioned for her to lead the way outside. She paused long enough to check that the stove and oven were off, then pulled on her coat and bonnet. She threw her shawl around her shoulders and took a deep breath before heading out with him into the storm.

She regretted her insistence the moment she stepped

outside and the howling wind tried to suck her breath right out of her mouth. Why had Becky Sue chosen such a horrible day to disappear? Closing her lips, Annie bent her head and pressed forward into the storm's unrelenting wall. She climbed into the buggy on one side while Caleb jumped in from the other. A single glance from him told her what she already knew.

If they didn't find Becky Sue soon, it might be too late.

Two hours later, half-frozen and wondering if he'd ever get feeling back in his hands, Caleb turned the open buggy toward the bakery. The storm was getting worse, and he couldn't risk a hit-or-miss search any longer. He'd alerted his neighbors, but none had seen the girl.

"Where are we headed?" Annie asked as she huddled beneath the trio of blankets they'd piled on top of themselves.

"To the bakery."

"To call the police?"

He was no longer surprised their minds worked in tandem. "I don't have any other choice. I don't want to delay any longer, and it's going to take longer to get back because of the snow."

"That isn't snow. It's ice." She whipped her scarf off and half turned to wrap the bright blue scarf around him. Looping a finger beneath the top edge, she pulled it up enough to cover the bottom half of his face. "Does that help?"

His voice was muffled as he replied, "Me, but you don't have any protection against the storm."

"I do." She raised her shawl up over her bonnet and held it closed in front of her nose.

He was about to argue, then noticed how tight the

stitches were in the thick wool shawl that reached almost to her knees. The wind would have to blow harder to drive the icy pellets past them.

"Did Leanna make your shawl?" he asked, to keep the conversation going. For some reason, it didn't feel as cold when they talked.

"No, I did."

"I didn't think you liked handicrafts."

"I don't like quilting, but I love to knit." Her laugh was muffled. "Last Christmas, I made scarves for everyone in the family. The *kinder* got ones with images of goats and ducks knit into them."

"They must have liked them."

"Rhoda says she doesn't have to insist on the *kinder* wearing their scarves when they go to school. They love wearing them."

He chuckled. "Sounds as if they were a great success. Maybe you should think of putting some out for sale at the bakery."

Her voice dropped to a near whisper. "I don't know if that's a *gut* idea."

"Why not?" He wondered why she always acted shy and withdrawn when he made a suggestion that would bring her more attention. "You've been talking about displaying Leanna's quilts. I think adding your scarves to the bakery's wares would add the color and interest to the space like you're always talking about." When she didn't reply, he kept his sigh silent. "Think about it. Okay?"

"Okay."

Why was she being so grudging? She'd offered him one idea after another, almost every one *gut*, and he was certain his customers would be interested in her hand-knit scarves.

When Annie remained silent, he put his arm around her shoulders and drew her closer so they could use each other's warmth to battle the wind. He was relieved to feel her shiver, because that meant she wasn't being overtaken by the cold yet. She was, he'd learned, far stronger than she looked.

Even so, she let him help her out when they got to the bakery. He left Dusty in a leeward spot, not wanting to unhitch the horse until he was sure when or if he'd be leaving the bakery tonight.

Keeping his arm around Annie, he lurched with her through the wind and into the bakery. They stopped inside the door, and Caleb reveled in taking a breath that wasn't snatched away by the storm.

He went to the phone and called 911. When someone picked up, it didn't take long to explain the situation. He was told the sheriff's department would send a deputy to the bakery as soon as possible.

"It may take a little longer than usual," the female dispatcher said. "Lots of accidents with the storm." She confirmed the bakery's address before hanging up.

Putting down the phone, he said, "Now we wait."

"The thing we hate most."

"Ja." There was nothing else he could say. She knew as well as he did how dangerous the weather was if Becky Sue hadn't been prepared for the storm.

Annie made hot chocolate while Caleb tested the fancy *kaffi* machine that he'd found in one of the crates delivered from the Summerhayses' house. He kept asking for her help to figure out the many buttons and attachments. She did her best to assist because she was grateful for anything to keep busy while they waited for the deputy to arrive. The ticking of the wall clock was a constant reminder of each passing minute. She kept listening for a vehicle to pull into the parking lot.

Even so, she recoiled when a heavy knock sounded on the front door. She went into the main room as Caleb hurried to answer the door. A man in a sheriff's department uniform stood on the other side.

The deputy sheriff thanked Caleb as he came inside. He wasn't as tall as Caleb, but his shaved head and grim expression warned he was all business. After a quick scan of the space, he introduced himself as Rick Flanagan. He nodded when Caleb gave him his name and hers. An offer of something warm to drink was waved aside by the deputy, and he got down to gathering information on why they'd called the sheriff's office.

The two men couldn't appear more different. Deputy Flanagan wore a uniform with a gun in a holster along with a myriad of other gadgets, and a radio and a camera hooked to his shoulder. Caleb's simple white shirt and black suspenders attached to his broadfall trousers announced he was a plain man who eschewed any sort of violence.

Yet both spoke with the same calm determination to resolve the problem. She wished she could be like them, but her heart was pounding as if trying to break out of her chest.

Could they find Becky Sue in time?

In silence, she watched. Deputy Flanagan listened to Caleb. The deputy nodded and wrote in a small notebook until Caleb said, "And that's all we know."

"A girl who's run away once will run again, I'm sorry to say. Miss Wagler, do you have anything to add?"

"No, sir. Other than I'm worried that she didn't run away."

"You believe someone may have forced her to go?"

"I can't believe she would leave her son behind if she'd had a choice."

The deputy nodded, but his face remained as free of emotion as the wall behind him. "You may have to make an official statement to that fact when we find her. Running away is very different from abandoning a child."

"She wouldn't do that," Annie asserted.

Deputy Flanagan unbent enough to give her a commiserating smile. "More kids who do stupid things need advocates like you in their corner. Let's find her and then we'll see what can be done to help her and her little boy." He flipped his notebook closed and stored it beneath his dark coat. "I know you plain folks don't keep photographs of each other, so I won't ask you for one. We'll go with the description you gave us."

Collecting their personal contact information, including the phone number for the bakery and when Caleb expected to be working there and when he'd be at his farm, Deputy Flanagan gave them each a card with his direct number on it.

"Don't hesitate to call," he said.

Caleb walked him to the door. After the deputy left, he turned off the *kaffi* machine.

Annie finished her hot chocolate and washed out the cup, looking over her shoulder when Caleb said, "It's beginning to snow harder, so we should get home."

"I wish there was more we could do," Annie said.

"We can pray for her safety. If we can't help, God can."

"I've already been doing that."

"Me, too." He smiled sadly. "I know this is upsetting for you, Annie, because it is for me. However, no matter how much we want to help, leaving Becky Sue in God's hands may be the best thing we can do."

"God and the sheriff's department."

"They work as part of His plan, too." He plucked her coat and black shawl off the peg and handed them to her. "Bundle up. If anything, it's got colder out."

"Impossible."

"I wish you were right."

She slipped her arms into her coat and hooked it closed before pulling the thick shawl over her shoulders.

"Do you think she knows that her parents don't want her to come home?" she asked as she watched him button his coat.

"She's a smart girl. She has to know about their disapproval." He gave an inelegant snort. "That's probably why she left."

"Will you insist she returns there after she's found?"

"It's my duty to see she's taken care of."

"And she's doing fine right here. Let's leave things the way they are until we've sorted out her story."

He shocked her by pulling her close and leaning his head against the top of her bonnet. She stiffened in astonishment, then softened against his firm chest as he murmured, "*Danki*, Annie. I don't know how I would have dealt with Becky Sue and Joey without you."

"You would have found a way. Caleb Hartz solves every problem." She tilted her head to look at him as she grinned. "Isn't that what everyone says?"

"If they did, they were wrong, because I couldn't have managed any of this without your help."

And my family's, she should have added, but she leaned her cheek on his chest again, savoring the moment that would never come again if her twin started walking out with him after the mud sale.

Chapter Thirteen

The wind eased as Caleb turned the buggy onto the twisting road that followed Harmony Creek because trees lined the road along the farm fences. The cold deepened more. He peered through the falling snow. He hadn't expected so many storms this late in the winter. Last winter had been rough, but had begun easing before the middle of March.

"Caleb! Look!"

At Annie's call, he shook himself out of his lethargy. Had he been surrendering to the cold? A fearsome thought.

Caleb peered through the thick snow in the direction she pointed. At his house, he realized. No, not the house. The driveway.

A gray-topped buggy was parked there. His buggy, he realized, when he saw the shelves stacked in the back seat. He'd planned to take them to the bakery until Becky Sue and the buggy vanished.

Turning into his drive, he didn't wait for the open buggy to stop before he jumped out. He raced through the fallen snow to his door.

He threw it open and stared at his young cousin, who was peeling an apple.

"Becky Sue, what are you doing here?"

"You said I could come here anytime I wanted," she replied, then waved as Annie came into the kitchen. "Hi, Annie! *Gut* to see you."

Caleb frowned. "But where have you been, Becky Sue? We've been looking everywhere for you."

"You were looking for me?" She kept her eyes on her task as she cut up the apple and dropped the slices onto others in a pie pan. "Why would you do that?"

"Because nobody knew where you were."

"You didn't?" She reached for a stick of butter and began to cut small slabs to put on top of the apples.

Annie stepped forward, pulling off her shawl. She dropped it on a chair. "You said you'd never leave without letting me or someone else know where you were going. You agreed to that, Becky Sue."

"I know, but we were talking about when I leave Harmony Creek."

He winced. How callously the girl spoke of walking away from the Waglers, who had welcomed her into their house and into their hearts!

"I thought," Annie said in a measured voice, "that you might have left Harmony Creek today."

"Without my son?"

"Ja."

Annie's terse answer had startled his cousin. Enough to stop her from acting as if everything that had happened was nothing more than an inadvertent misunderstanding?

"I wouldn't leave my son like that," Becky Sue said. "I love him."

"We know you do," Caleb replied with care. "Anyone who sees the two of you together knows that you belong together."

His cousin made a soft sound. A gulp? A gasp? A smothered sob? He couldn't tell as she put the top crust on the pie.

"I left you a note on the table in the living room at your house, Annie." At last, Becky Sue looked at them. "Right by the books Leanna is always reading."

"But Leanna was at her job, and I was at the bakery."

"Oh," Becky Sue said with a flippant shrug. "I guess that's why you didn't see it. I thought you were home when I went out."

"Out where?" He regretted the question before Annie put a cautionary hand on his arm. The minute the words came out of his mouth, Becky Sue's face grew stony.

"We've been worried about you," Annie said. "If we sound angry, it's because we were scared you'd got lost in the storm."

"I know to stay in on a bad day like this." The girl waved the knife she was using to slice openings in the top crust. "I mean, I came over here, but it can't be a half mile from your house to here, Annie." Lowering the knife to the counter, she sighed. "Okay, I came over here to make a couple pies for you, Caleb. I thought if you sampled what I can bake, you might hire me to work in your bakery, too."

He hoped he was able to hide his shock. The last thing he wanted in his bakery was a recalcitrant teenager who seldom thought of anything but herself.

Again Annie saved him from saying something he'd regret. "Becky Sue, I'm sure once Caleb's bakery is the success it's going to be, he'll be looking to hire several more people. How wise of you to look toward the future like that!"

If there was sarcasm behind her comment, he didn't hear it. Neither did the girl, because she smiled and carried the pie to the oven.

He left the two in his house as he went to the phone shack between his house and Jeremiah's. A quick call to Deputy Flanagan put a halt to the search for Becky Sue. Yet Caleb remained bothered by something he couldn't explain.

After he'd dropped Annie off at her house and he was on his way home, Caleb realized what had been nettling him. If his cousin had left a note on the living room table by the books, one of the Waglers would have seen it. He couldn't imagine *Grossmammi* Inez's eagle eyes not picking up on something as unusual as a note left on a table in the living room.

Becky Sue had been lying…again.

Annie followed Caleb into the bakery the next morning. He'd told her on the ride from her house that he'd checked out the colors she'd painted on the wall, and he thought her idea of yellow would be the best. She listened to his comments, knowing he didn't want to talk about Becky Sue and what had happened yesterday. Like her, he didn't believe a note had been left at her house. There hadn't been any sign of it last night, and Becky Sue's excuse was that the *boppli* or the puppy might have taken it.

Caleb groaned as he halted right in front of her.

She squeezed past him and stared at the front room in shock. Paint was splattered over every surface and flowed across the floor, mixing together in puddles in the scraped boards. The whole space looked as if a rainbow had exploded in it.

"What happened?" he asked, shock straining his voice.

As if in answer to his question, Joey began to shriek from the other side of the display case.

Annie ran around the case to where the little boy stood. He held two paintbrushes, one in each hand. They dragged on the floor, adding another layer of paint to the worn wood. Blue and yellow were speckled across his clothing and in his hair.

She waved Caleb away, and he stepped into the kitchen. Once he was out of sight, the little boy's tears vanished. When she knelt beside him, Joey reached out to pat her face. He began to grin, his six teeth, including the new ones, visible.

"Jo-Jo. Pretty."

Annie picked up the *boppli* and stood before he could do more damage. She took the paintbrushes from him. When he started to screw up his face again to protest, she said, "It's very, very pretty, Joey, but it's finished."

"Fin-ish?"

She used the word he did at the end of every meal. "Done. You did a *gut* job."

That was the truth, she had to acknowledge. There weren't many surfaces he hadn't painted. The glass in the display case was covered with streaks of yellow, blue and green from the small sample bottles they'd got from the hardware store, and the front door had those colors as well as red—where had that paint come from?—which were marked on it with tiny fingerprints.

Puddles of paint marked any lower area in the floor. More paint oozed in slow streams around higher ridges in the wood, creating a crazy-quilt pattern.

She was relieved to see that the big window hadn't been splashed, but there was a spot of red on the ceiling near the door. How had the toddler managed to get paint up there?

Looking at the kitchen, she said nothing as she watched Caleb take in what one small boy had done in such a short time. It couldn't have taken him long because Becky Sue was an attentive *mamm*, keeping a close eye on her son.

At that thought, Annie asked, "Where's your *mamm*?"

The bathroom door opened and Becky Sue emerged. She stared around herself in disbelief. "Joey did this?"

Annie frowned. Was it possible for a single one-year-old *boppli* to make such a mess so quickly? She bit back her question as tears welled up in Becky's eyes.

"Oh, Caleb," the girl cried. "I'm sorry. I left him alone for just a moment while I was in the bathroom. I never guessed he could do this! I'll clean it up."

"No, get him out of here."

Her face crumbled. "Caleb, I'm so, so sorry. Please don't be angry."

"I'm not, but you need to get out of here."

Tears rolled down her cheeks. "We shouldn't have come to Harmony Creek Hollow. We've caused you nothing but trouble. I hope you can forgive me. You've got to forgive Joey."

"Becky Sue, you're misunderstanding me." His voice softened as he put a hand on his cousin's shoulder. "I don't want you to leave the settlement. I want you to get Joey out of the bakery because I don't know how old that red paint is. It might have lead in it. A little one shouldn't be near that stuff." He gave her a gentle smile. "There's nothing to forgive. As my teacher used to say, boys will be boys and nothing on God's green earth will ever change that."

Annie's heart swelled at how kind he was to the distraught girl. She hurried to add, "Don't worry, Becky Sue. Caleb and I will take care of this." She held out the little boy, making sure he didn't face his cousin and start crying again.

Taking him, Becky Sue said, "But it'll take you hours to clean this up."

"Which is why we must get started."

The girl nodded, gathered her son to her and, holding his face against his shoulder so he didn't see Caleb, hurried to get them into their coats and out of the bakery.

As soon as they were gone, Annie carried the paintbrushes to the bathroom so she could rinse them out in the old sink. Caleb called after her, and she halted.

"I couldn't hear everything she said from the kitchen," he said. "Did she explain why she was here?"

"No." She looked at the back door. "What do you think she's up to?"

Caleb found the top for the yellow paint container and twisted it on. Setting it on top of the green jar, he said, "I can't begin to guess what goes on in Becky Sue's head." He glanced around the mess the *boppli* had made. "To think I took so long making up my mind about what colors I wanted in my bakery."

A laugh burst out of Annie. She clamped her hand over her mouth, but whimsy continued to spark in her eyes. After putting the brushes in a cup in the sink and running water in it, she said, "I'm sorry, Caleb. I know it isn't funny."

"You're right. It isn't funny." He bent and ran his finger through a blob of yellow paint. "But this is." He tapped the end of her pert nose with his fingertip.

She yelped. "What did you do that for?"

"So your face matches your apron."

Looking at the splotches of color on her black apron, she laughed. She got a cloth and cleaned her nose. "You know, Caleb, the walls can be repainted, but…"

"But what?"

"What do you think of leaving the floor as it is? It looks so cheerful."

He had to agree. "But too fancy for a bakery run by plain folks. I doubt our leaders would think it's appropriate."

"You could ask Eli and Jeremiah." She got another clean rag and began to wipe the paint from the glass display case. "There's nothing in our *Ordnung* about a painted floor in a retail shop."

"True."

"And you can tell them that the design was Joey's idea."

"*A little child shall lead them*, it says in Isaiah, though that's not the intention of the verse."

"Why not?" She chuckled. "If we leave his fingerprints right next to the splatters, it'll be clear to everyone that youthful enthusiasm created this. Who knows? People may come from far and wide to take a look at your floor."

"I'd rather have them come for the baked goods."

"They'll come *back* for those." Rinsing out the cloth in the sink, she patted his arm as she walked past him to get a bucket from the kitchen. "You worry too much, Caleb. Trust God will see you through."

"I do trust God, but He has left the details to me."

"You worry too much," she repeated. "You should try to enjoy watching your dream come true."

Her words stung. Not because they weren't true, because her advice was sound. However, her words reminded him of Verba and her constant harping that he should be different from what he was. He hadn't guessed that Verba's meddling would still bother him, but it did. It took all his strength to submerge those feelings and not lash out with serrated words, because it wasn't Annie's fault he couldn't get over what Verba had done. Until he could, he must not consider walking out with any other woman.

Not even, he thought as he watched Annie fill the bucket in the kitchen sink, this one.

Why couldn't she guard her tongue and halt it from wagging before she had a chance to think?

Annie dumped yet another bucket of paint-filled water into the kitchen sink, being careful not to splash the dirty water onto the counter and cabinets. Her fingers clenched on its plastic side. How could she lecture Caleb, who was a man of great faith? So many people had hoped he would marry before the men in their settlement were ordained, because they'd hoped that he would go from their community leader to their spiritual leader. His ability to listen to both sides and find common ground was admired. By the *Leit* and *Englischers*, according to what she'd heard his fellow volunteer firemen say.

She tried to engage him in conversation while they worked to clean the cases, the ceiling and the walls. Every attempt failed. He'd respond with a few words, then go quiet. As the morning passed, she wondered if he'd said more than a dozen complete sentences to her.

When, a couple of hours after midday, Caleb said that they should return in the morning and start the repainting then, she was relieved. She rinsed out the cloths and bucket she'd used, as well as the paintbrushes Joey had. She hadn't seen where Caleb had put the paint containers. She guessed they were somewhere out of reach of the little boy.

How had Joey managed to open the containers? She was plagued by the niggling thought that he hadn't managed it on his own, but she couldn't guess why Becky Sue would help her son make such a mess.

Annie wished she and Caleb could discuss it, but he'd raised a high wall between them with his curt answers and silences. She finished cleaning up before pulling on her coat and other outerwear.

The ride to her house was as uncomfortable as the work at the shop. When she got out of the buggy, she thanked Caleb as she did each day and told him she'd see him tomorrow. He nodded and turned the buggy toward the road.

Shouts rang through the air. Happy shouts. She glanced toward the far end of the hollow. It sounded like teenagers having a *gut* time. With a sigh, she walked toward the house.

Squealing tires and a scream vanished beneath a crash that reverberated through the winter afternoon. The huge snowbanks couldn't muffle it.

Annie whirled. A buggy was crumpled against a tree. Caleb's? No, he'd been going in the other direction. She ran toward it.

The cold lashed at her. She paid it no mind. She heard shouts from the barn behind her, but didn't slow as she ran out onto the road.

A car appeared over a hill, racing in her direction. She scrambled toward a snowbank. The car skidded right in front of her. She tumbled forward and stared at its out-of-control bumper coming toward her.

Hands grasped her arms. She was yanked up the bank and away from the car. Snow spurted from beneath the tires, pelting her. She heard a deep grunt and knew the icy shards had also struck the person who'd pulled her out of the way. They collapsed together into the softer snow on the far side of the snowbank.

"Are you hurt?" she heard from beside her.

Caleb!

She glanced toward the drive where his buggy stood just down the road, safe.

Caleb had pulled her away from the car. He'd saved her from injury, possibly from being killed.

She longed to throw her arms around him and press her face to his chest while she thanked him over and over for saving her life. She couldn't. For so many, many reasons, but the most important was that Lyndon and Juanita were hurrying at their best possible speed through the snow toward them.

"I'm fine." *Thanks to you.* She was surprised how the idea of saying those words made her feel so shy. "How are you?"

"I'm okay, Annie."

"What happened?" shouted Lyndon.

As one, she and Caleb stood and looked in the direction the shouts had come from.

Annie didn't wait to answer her brother's question. She slid over the snowbank and down to the road. Racing along it, she reached the broken buggy. The horse was being cut loose by a teenage boy, and the mare pressed against the snow as it raced past her, panicked but unhurt.

Two more boys were standing behind the buggy. They were staring at the snow. Not by the buggy, but by a tree several feet beyond it.

She gasped when she saw another boy lying in the snow next to the tree. She recognized the groan she'd heard too often when her younger brother didn't want to do chores.

Running up to him, she pushed past the boys. "Kenny, are you okay?"

"Ja." The word, spoken through his cracked and bleeding lips, wasn't reassuring, but he pushed himself to his feet. He winced when he bent to pick up what she realized were broken skis. Limping, he hobbled to where Caleb had reached the boys by the ruined buggy.

The boys let out a worried yell when Kenny's knees folded beneath him and he fell, face-first, into the snow.

Rolling Kenny onto his back, Caleb motioned the rest of them to stand aside. He swept snow off her brother's face before running his hands along Kenny's arms and legs, then his torso. Though unconscious, Kenny winced when Caleb touched his left side.

"I'd say he's cracked a rib or two." Caleb motioned to the boys. "Go to the nearest phone and call 911. Tell them to send an ambulance."

"Go!" Annie ordered when the boys seemed unable to move.

They rushed away.

Not wanting to leave Kenny in the snow and risk hypothermia, Caleb and Lyndon tore the seat out of the buggy and slid it beneath the boy. Annie dug in the broken buggy and found a blanket, which she draped over him, then she watched as they carried Kenny to the house.

The next two hours were a blur as the rescue squad came and the two EMTs checked over Kenny, who'd regained his senses by the time he was inside the house. The EMTs agreed with Caleb's diagnosis and suggested taking Kenny for X-rays. However, *Grossmammi* Inez decided that, because the emergency room was more than thirty miles away, it wasn't worth putting him through the uncomfortable ride on roads filled with potholes. They wrapped his ribs and suggested Kenny see the local *doktor* tomorrow.

One of the EMTs let Annie use his cell phone to make the appointment before they packed up their supplies and left, each with a bag of chocolate chip cookies and a jar of chowchow. Becky Sue had put together the food while everyone else hovered around Kenny's room.

The teen asked if she could see how he was doing, and Annie said, "You're going to have to wait. He's sleeping, but when he wakes he'll be bored. Maybe you can take Joey in and spend some time with him."

"Joey likes your brother."

"And my brother likes him." She smiled. "I think he's glad for once not to be the youngest guy around the house."

Becky Sue chuckled. "I'll put together some blocks and books for Joey. That way they can entertain each other."

"And give you some time to catch up on the mending you need to do."

The girl's nose wrinkled in disgust. "I hate mending."

"Me, too," she said, copying Becky Sue's expression.

Again the girl laughed, and Annie suspected she was seeing a bit of the person Becky Sue would have been if she didn't hide her true self among so many secrets.

Coming down the stairs, Annie saw Caleb pacing in the kitchen. He'd remained there after bringing Kenny in, not wanting to upset Joey.

"Kenny is going to be fine," she said before he could ask. "*Danki* for helping."

He ignored her gratitude as she'd known he would. "Did he mention what happened?"

"They were buggy skiing." She shook her head in amazement. "One of the boys spent some time on the internet at the library and saw other plain kids skiing behind a buggy. They thought it would be fun, and I'm sure it was."

"Until a car came speeding along the road. Most likely, more kids out for what they considered fun."

"The driving is becoming more reckless. They're drag racing before it gets dark."

He sighed and reached for his hat. "We're going to have to talk with the sheriff's office again. Not that it'll do much *gut*. They'll patrol for a few weeks, and the kids will lie low. As soon as the patrols ease off, the drag racing begins again."

"It's all we can do. The rest is in God's hands."

"You have such a solid faith," he said with a smile.

"Some days. Others it's as wobbly as Kenny on his skis." She came around the table. "That's why we call it faith, ain't so? Because we have to depend on it no matter how sure we feel about anything."

"Are you okay?"

"I'm fine." She held up a finger. "And before you ask, everyone else is, too. Leanna is keeping a close eye on our *grossmammi*, and Becky Sue is going to sit with Kenny when he wakes up."

"The two of them alone?"

She laughed, "You sound like a suspicious *daed*, Caleb. Don't worry. To Kenny, your cousin is a much older woman. He's twelve, and the only females he's interested in spending time with are the calves he hopes to raise to add to our dairy herd." Her voice softened. "Don't look for trouble where there isn't any."

"You're right."

When he closed the distance between them with a couple of long steps, she knew she should back away, find an excuse to head upstairs before…

Before what?

Before he reached out to her, or before she stepped forward and drew his arms around herself? She yearned to feel the strength that had hefted her brother and carried him through the snow to their house. How much joy would there have been in that powerful, yet gentle, embrace?

The answers weren't for her to find. Leanna was the one who should be in his arms, not her. Pain rushed through her, so potent that a gasp slipped past her lips. When Caleb asked her what was wrong, she shook her head.

Was *this* what Leanna had been feeling since Gabriel Miller abandoned her to marry someone else?

No, that must be worse, because Leanna had been in love with Gabriel. What Annie felt for Caleb was… She didn't know, but she was certain of one thing. She would do whatever she could so her sister didn't have to feel such sorrow again.

Stepping away from him before she could no longer resist the invitation in his eyes, she bade him a *gut nacht* in a strangled voice.

"Annie, what's wrong?" he asked again.

She wouldn't lie and tell him that everything was fine. But she couldn't speak of the tempest within her, a storm pulling her this way and that like a maniacal tornado.

"Gut nacht," she said again.

He took the hint and left.

She sank to sit at the table, her face in her hands.

How much longer could she bear being torn apart by her longings, which were in opposition to one another? She had to bring this to an end.

But how? Next week, Leanna would be spending the whole day with Caleb, and Annie would be as lost as she'd ever been. Because she couldn't pretend to herself any longer. She might not be joining her sister and Caleb, but her heart would be because somewhere, sometime, when she hadn't realized it, she'd given it to him.

Chapter Fourteen

Annie smiled when her twin sister came into the kitchen the morning of the mud sale. Breakfast wasn't ready yet. She'd been serving it later the past week. Until Kenny's ribs healed, he couldn't help in the barn. Lyndon was doing the milking alone, and he had twice as many cows as most plain farmers did. Other farmers and their *kinder* who were old enough to help came when they could. Leanna had pitched in, but not today when she didn't want to go to the mud sale smelling of animals and hay.

"Gute mariye," Leanna said. She couldn't hide her excitement about the day ahead. No wonder. Not only was she going to the Salem Volunteer Department's first ever mud sale—something that the firefighters already hoped would become an annual event—but she was going to spend the day with Caleb.

Though Annie wanted to thank God for offering her twin sister the chance to have time with a man she was attracted to, the words wouldn't come. She hoped her envy was hidden.

"You look lovely." Annie brushed a bit of lint from her sister's dark cranberry-colored sleeve. She wondered when Leanna had managed to make a new dress as well as finish up the quilt she'd donated.

"For a mud sale?" Leanna laughed. "They didn't get their name because we're expected to dress in our best."

"Then maybe I should have said you look as if you're anticipating having a great day."

"I hope for Caleb's sake—and for the sake of the firefighters—that it's going to be a great day. From what you and Lyndon have said, they've been working hard to make it the best mud sale ever."

"That's why Caleb's been exhausted the past week. Working on the mud sale and his farm and the bakery."

"That's opening soon, ain't so?"

"The first week of May."

Leanna plucked her bonnet off its peg. "So you'll be trading your paintbrush for cookie cutters."

"I don't know how much baking I'll be doing."

Caleb hadn't said, and she hadn't asked. Becky Sue had come to the bakery a few days ago and had prepared several more pies and batches of cookies to show him what she could do. The teen was an excellent baker, and though Caleb had said nothing, Annie suspected his cousin would be working at least part-time in the kitchen once the bakery opened its doors.

That would be for the best, she'd told herself over and over. With Becky Sue present, she and Caleb wouldn't be alone as they'd been for the past few weeks. The timing was perfect if he and Leanna started walking out after their day together. God knew what He was doing.

Oh, if only she did.

"Caleb's buggy's coming up the drive," Leanna said, breaking into Annie's thoughts as she opened the door. "I'll see you there."

"I hope so."

Leanna frowned. "I shouldn't go with Caleb. He'll understand."

"Go ahead. *Grossmammi* Inez seems to be in *gut* spirits and was breathing better yesterday. Maybe she's right, and her symptoms are just left over from her cold." Annie longed to believe that, but feared there was something else wrong with her *grossmammi*. "I don't want you to miss the quilt auction."

"Our *grossmammi* is more important than seeing who buys my quilt."

Annie made shooing motions. "Go! You don't want to make Caleb late."

Blowing her sister a kiss, Leanna rushed out the door.

As the door closed, Annie's smile fell away. She bit her lower lip, refusing to let the tears burning her eyes fall. Wasn't this what she'd been working for? Leanna had been smiling as she left. Annie hadn't seen her sister look so happy since the news of Gabriel's marriage.

"You should have gone with them" came her *grossmammi*'s voice from behind her.

Annie spun to assist *Grossmammi* Inez to the table. "I didn't realize you were up already."

"I've been awake for a couple of hours." She looked past Annie toward where a buggy was visible through the windows that gave a view of the road. "I hope you are sure of what you are doing."

"Doing?"

"Matchmaking." She sat at the table. "Be careful about matchmaking for your sister and Caleb. Your own heart is too involved, and it may keep you from seeing what's right in front of you."

"I know." Annie sat facing her *grossmammi*. "But if there's a chance Leanna will be happy again—"

"That is God's choice and hers."

At *Grossmammi* Inez's tone, Annie didn't argue further. What could she say? She was on a treacherous path, a path that might not be the one God had for her or for her sister, but she didn't know how to step off.

Annie smiled at Joey, who sat in the middle of the kitchen floor. When he dropped to his belly to crawl to a block that had fallen off the pile he was gathering, she tried not to laugh while he groped to grab it and pull it to where his toes touched the other blocks.

"You're a cute little worm," she said as she finished drying the last of the dishes from breakfast.

He looked at her with his grin that showed several more teeth that had popped up during the past week. After days of misery, he was content again. But he had sniffles, and Becky Sue hadn't wanted him to go to the mud sale. The teenager had been thrilled when Annie volunteered to stay home with the *boppli* while she joined the rest of the Waglers—including Kenny, who promised to sit quietly—at the mud sale.

Grossmammi Inez had aimed a knowing glance at Annie when she left with the others. The older woman thought that Annie was hiding at home so she didn't have to see her twin with Caleb. Again, it was something Annie couldn't argue with because it was the truth.

But spending time with the *boppli* had been delightful. Every time she looked at him she thought of how adorable he'd looked while covered with paint at the bakery. He was a *gut* little boy, willing to entertain himself. If only he didn't panic when he saw Caleb... Joey went to her brother and to Jeremiah and to Eli and to the Kuhns brothers. The list went on and on.

A pair of blocks tumbled away. Again Joey stretched out, keeping his foot on the pile while he reached for a block. He swept his hands along the floor, missing the other block.

Annie gasped as she watched the *boppli* reaching as far as he could, again running his hand along the floor. But he misjudged, and he missed the block a second time. Frustrated, he cradled the block he'd found.

Was it possible that the little boy couldn't see well? She thought of the times he'd touched her face as if confirming what his eyes failed to show him.

Tiptoeing around the *kind*, she picked up a ball with a bell in it. She kept it silent and knelt an arm's length away. She held up the ball to his left and rang it.

Joey's head swiveled toward it. To his right, she rocked his favorite blue bear. He didn't look at it. She shifted the bell to his right side and shook it again. His head shifted, but he didn't reach for his beloved bear though it was about eighteen inches from his face.

She moved it closer. When it was about two inches from his face, Joey chortled. "Bear-bear." He grabbed for it with such excitement she knew he hadn't seen it until then.

Annie handed him the bear and let her hands fall to her lap. She watched as he pressed his nose to it and repeated its name as he did each time one of them picked him up.

Her head spun. The little boy couldn't see past the end of his nose. That explained why he preferred to pull himself along on his belly than get up on his hands and knees or walk. So close to the floor, he was able to perceive what was right in front of him.

Was there a way for a *doktor* to test his ability to see? If it were possible, were there glasses small enough for a *boppli*?

But it wasn't her decision to make. She must talk to

Becky Sue before she did anything. She hoped that this time the girl would listen to *gut* sense.

Again she gasped as she realized something else. None of the men Joey went to had hair as light as Caleb's. Was the *kind* confusing Caleb for someone else? She wrapped her arms around herself as she wondered if that other person was the reason Becky Sue had run away.

Annie must talk to Caleb and get his insight on how best to break the news to his cousin. None of this was going to be easy, but this was one secret they couldn't keep. Joey had to have help, and she guessed Becky Sue did, too.

Caleb took an appreciative bite of his second hot dog. There was almost as much relish as meat in the roll, and he savored it. Leanna sat beside him near one of the propane torches that fought back the cold outside the auction tent. She ate her hamburger much more delicately than he was wolfing down his lunch.

"How's your burger?" he asked.

"It's *gut*. I can tell you like hot dogs."

"Pretty obvious, ain't so?" He was pleased that she was beginning to get more comfortable with him. For the first hour, while they sat in the bleachers under the big white tent behind the fire station, she hadn't said a word.

He'd thought she'd voice her opinion of some of the animals being auctioned off, but she hadn't spoken. She'd watched as each lot was sold, though she'd leaned forward when two lots of goats came under the hammer.

The mud sale was going well, as far as he could see. There was a single auctioneer at a time instead of the usual two or three he'd seen at the mud sales in Lancaster County, where there were many more donations after years of the events. But the firefighters were pleased with the amount of goods they'd received and how much money was being raised. Several lots had been sold for more than they were worth, which meant there were many generous souls in the crowd that was bigger than Caleb had hoped because the temperature seemed more like mid-January than early April.

Leanna's intricate nine-square quilt, in shades of cranberry, green and off-white, had sold for almost two thousand dollars because a pair of *Englisch* women had pushed the price higher and higher until one gave up. As soon as the next item came up for bid, the loser sought out Leanna and asked if she could hire Leanna to make her a similar quilt. Leanna had agreed to do so for the price of the materials and a donation to the fire department of the same amount as the other woman had paid.

"That was generous of you to agree to make the second quilt," Caleb said, hoping to keep the conversation going. How could it be so easy to talk with Annie while it felt as if he had to wrest every word out of Leanna?

"I'm honored to be able to help the fire department." Leanna took another bite of her burger and dabbed her napkin at the ketchup clinging to her lips.

Caleb watched her motions. How could her mouth be so like her twin sister's, but he wasn't tempted to taste it as he was Annie's?

When she caught him staring at her, he rushed to say, "You know Chief Pulaski is going to hope you'll donate another quilt next year."

"I plan to. I enjoy putting the pieces together. There's something about a quilt pattern that brings sense to an otherwise chaotic world." She flushed as if she'd revealed too much. "Sorry. You don't want to hear about my quilting."

"Nonsense. I understand how you feel. Being in the kitchen gives me the same feeling of peace."

She smiled at last. "You do understand. I'm glad." She paused, then asked, "My sister talked you into bringing me here today, ain't so?"

"Why do you say that?"

"Because I know my sister better than I know anyone else in the world." Leanna's gentle laugh told him she wasn't upset by Annie's matchmaking. "I've seen how she looks at me when she thinks I don't see. She's determined to make me happy, no matter what."

"And you're not happy being here today?"

"I'm having a *wunderbaar* time, Caleb. Not as she'd hoped, though."

"What do you mean?"

"You're a very nice man, and your sister is one of my best friends in the whole world, but I know you don't have any interest in me beyond being friends."

"Or you in me?"

"That's a loaded question."

He shook his head. "Don't worry what you say will hurt my feelings because, to be honest, Leanna, you're a very nice woman, and my sister is also one of my best friends in the whole world."

When she didn't laugh as he'd anticipated, he wondered if, despite the forthrightness she seldom revealed, he'd insulted her. He realized he'd misinterpreted her silence when she spoke again after he put the papers from their food in a trash barrel.

"What about *my* sister?" she asked. "Do you consider her a friend, too?"

It was his turn to be silent. Friend? Was that how he'd describe what he felt about Annie? Friend seemed too tepid when he thought about the fiery woman. And he'd be a *dummkopf* to pretend he didn't want more with Annie.

But not now, he started to tell himself as he had so often. This time the words wouldn't come. He didn't want to lie to himself any longer. He wanted to put his past behind him and look to the future. A future with Annie.

Leanna chuckled, and when he looked at her, he saw she was grinning. His thoughts must have been visible, no surprise when such a big revelation struck him.

"You don't have to answer," Leanna said, patting his arm as she stood. "But I do have one important request. Please don't hurt my sister as her last boyfriend did."

"Last boyfriend?" He was amazed at the rush of anger that filled him at the thought of someone hurting Annie. "What did he do?"

"It's not my place to say. If Annie wants you to know, she'll tell you." With another smile, Leanna walked away toward where her *grossmammi* and brothers were talking with some *Englischers* he didn't recognize.

His heart thudded with anticipation; then he realized Annie wasn't with them. Hadn't she come to the mud sale? He stood and began to walk through the crowd. If she was there, he intended to find her. It was long past time that he spoke from his heart.

The kitchen door opening roused Annie, who was somewhere between awake and sleeping. Raising her head from her arms folded on the table, she smiled at her twin.

"Did I wake you?" Leanna asked.

"No. I was almost asleep, but not quite. Everyone else came home about two hours ago." Her words were interrupted by a wide yawn. "Did you have a *gut* time?"

"I did."

Annie almost mentioned what she'd discovered about Joey's sight, but halted herself. She must tell Caleb first so they could inform Becky Sue together. After that, the rest of the family and the *Leit* would be told.

"I thought you were coming to the mud sale today, too."

"Didn't Becky Sue tell you why I stayed behind?"

"She did. That was kind of you, Annie."

Embarrassed by her sister's praise, she asked, "Did the auction go well?"

"From what Lyndon was told by the fire chief, they're guessing that the fire department made as much or more than they do from their annual Fourth of July carnival."

"That's so *gut* to hear."

"I saw several volunteers thanking Caleb for giving them the idea of holding the auction and sale."

"Did you have fun with him?"

"We did, but after lunch we went our own ways."

Shocked, Annie blurted, "You did? So, who brought you home?"

"Sarah's brothers."

Annie was astonished. Menno and Benjamin Kuhns were two of the most hardworking men among the *Leit*, running a sawmill and a Christmas tree farm while planting an apple orchard on another of the steep hills behind their house. She wondered if one or both were interested in her sister, but she was more curious why Leanna hadn't spent the whole day with Caleb.

Before she could ask, her sister went on, "We talked about having a skating party tomorrow night on their pond. Will you come, Annie?"

Ach, how she wished Caleb had been the one to ask, but she would be a fool to keep hoping for something that wasn't going to happen.

"It sounds like fun," she said.

"Probably more fun than I had today with Caleb."

Annie sat straighter. "Did something go wrong?"

Pulling out a chair across from her, Leanna smiled. "Of course not. I had a nice day watching the sale and listening to Caleb talk about the bakery."

"He's so excited that it's going to open next month. Did he tell you about his plans for opening day?"

"No, because he spent most of our time together talking about you."

"Me?"

Leanna reached across the table and clasped Annie's hand in hers. "For someone who's so smart and has so many *wunderbaar* ideas, Annie, you don't have a clue to what's right in front of your eyes. He's not interested in walking out with me, and I'm not interested in walking out with him."

"He told you that?"

"Ja." She smiled. "You did us a favor, Annie. Today showed us—both of us—that we can be friends. Nothing more."

"Are you sure? I know he's not similar to Gabriel—"

"Gabriel has nothing to do with any of this."

Annie doubted that, but didn't want to quarrel with her sister.

"He's not interested in me, Annie, because he's interested in you."

"Me?" Her voice squeaked as she repeated the single word.

"Ja. You think I'm lost in my grief over losing Gabriel. It's true the hurt remains, but how many more years are you going to hide behind your betrayal after what Rolan did to you?" She squeezed Annie's hand, then stood. "You've always been the brave one, Annie, the one who dares to speak her mind. Do you have enough courage to take another chance on love?"

Chapter Fifteen

It should have been like any of the other days that Caleb had come to the Waglers' house to pick up Annie so they could ride together to work at the bakery.

It wasn't.

He was exhausted from tossing and turning, checking his bedside clock every few minutes in the hope that dawn was near. Leanna's voice echoed in his mind: *But I do have one important request. Please don't hurt my sister as her last boyfriend did.*

Doing Annie any injury was the last thing he wanted. Despite not knowing what her ex had done, he wanted to see Annie's scintillating smile and listen to her excitement when she offered up yet another idea. If he had his way, she'd never be sad ever again. That wasn't realistic, but his heart didn't care. Its yearning was to be given in to her care.

Was that why he felt as nervous as a new scholar on the first day of school when he jumped out of his buggy? Only the kitchen lights were on, and he guessed the family was sleeping later after a busy day at the mud sale. A glance at Lyndon's house showed it was dark, too, but the barn glowed. Milking couldn't be delayed because someone had had a long day the day before.

Walking into the kitchen, he started to greet Annie, who was reaching for a bowl on an upper shelf. Joey stood behind her, unsteady on his feet, groping toward the top of the stove where oatmeal bubbled in a pot.

Caleb exploded across the kitchen, scooping up the *boppli* and swinging him away from the stove before his little fingers were burned. Joey let out a cry of surprise as if he couldn't figure out how he went from standing on his own two feet to having them sway twice his height above the floor.

"Turn him around, Caleb!" Annie ordered.

"What?" Caleb looked at her.

"Turn him around, Caleb! Now!"

"He'll scream once he sees who's holding him."

"Turn him around and hold him nose to nose."

"What?"

Annie was usually so pragmatic. Why was she acting crazy?

"Do it, Caleb!"

Not sure what she meant, he shifted the *kind* so Joey was facing him.

"Nose to nose," Annie urged. "Do it, Caleb! Fast!"

Lifting the *boppli* higher, Caleb felt like a *dummkopf* when he put the tip of his nose against Joey's tiny one. He steeled himself for the screech that would batter his ears.

But the little boy didn't scream. Joey regarded him with dark green eyes much like Caleb's own, then gave him a big grin.

When the *kind* reached up and ran his fingers along Caleb's face as he'd done to others, Caleb's breath hitched. Was the *boppli* accepting him? Tears blurred his distorted view of Joey's face as the toddler began to chortle as he repeated something that sounded like "Kay-eb" over and over.

"He's trying to say your name," Annie said.

"He's not crying." Caleb chuckled when the little boy continued to pat his face.

"Because he can see you."

He looked past the *kind* to where Annie stood by the stove. She wasn't smiling. When she outlined what she suspected about Joey's vision, he listened without comment until she mentioned that she believed the *boppli* had mistaken him for someone else, someone who had treated him poorly.

When she took Joey and put him in his high chair, where pieces of toast waited on the tray, Caleb struggled to dampen his rage. Who would have frightened a little *kind* so?

"Do you think it's why Becky Sue...?" He let his voice trail off when his cousin walked into the kitchen, rubbing sleep from her eyes.

"What about me?" she asked before looking from him to her son. "He's not crying!"

Annie put a hand on Caleb's shoulder as she said, "He knows Caleb isn't the person who's scared him."

The teenager shuddered before stiffening her shoulders. "I don't know what you mean."

Caleb went around the table to stand in front of his cousin. "I think you do, Becky Sue."

Behind him, Joey kept repeating his name in a singsong voice before giggling with obvious joy.

Becky Sue moved to collect her son, but Annie stepped between her and the high chair.

"I don't know," Annie said quietly, "how to tell you this other than straight out. Joey should be examined by an eye *doktor*. He can't see more than an inch or two in front of his face."

The girl's face lost color. "No, that's impossible."

"It's possible, and it's true." Annie's voice remained gentle. "I discovered it yesterday while you were at the mud sale. It was confirmed when Caleb held Joey close enough so your son could see his face. We'll get him to see a *doktor* who can help him. *Doktors* can do marvelous things, so they should be able to help him."

Caleb interjected, "Say the word, Becky Sue, and I'll make an appointment for him. Once we know what's wrong and what can be done, then we can talk about the other issue."

With a brokenhearted cry, the girl snatched the *boppli* from the chair and sped out of the room.

"Let me," Caleb said as Becky Sue's footsteps pounded up the stairs.

"I'll show you where to go," Annie replied.

He followed her upstairs. When she pointed to the second door on the left, he nodded and walked toward it. He paused at the door, unsure if he should enter the room his cousin shared with Annie.

"Go ahead," Annie murmured from behind him. "You must talk with her. I'll wait out here."

He gave her a quick nod, took a deep breath and went into the room that didn't look so different from the one where he slept. Though there were two narrow beds instead of his broad one, they were covered with handmade quilts as his was. Joey's crib, where the little boy was cuddling a blue teddy bear and babbling to it as if it understood him, sat in a spot where, in his own room, Caleb had placed a dower chest that had been in his family since their arrival in America over two hundred and fifty years before. The same green shades as in his room could be drawn to keep out the sun, and rag rugs warmed the oak floors.

Becky Sue looked up at him from where she sat on the bed closer to the crib. She didn't say a word, but seemed to withdraw into herself like a turtle pulling into its shell.

Deciding to take a cue from Annie, he cut to the heart of the matter. "I don't know what I've done to make you distrust me so much."

"You haven't done anything."

"Then why are you upset that Joey didn't shriek today when I was holding him? I'd have thought you'd be glad, too, that he isn't terrified of me any longer. What's wrong?"

She stared at her folded hands. "I can't say."

"Can't or won't?"

"Isn't that the same?"

Not wanting to get into another discussion with her that would go in circles and never get to the point, he said, "You've been here over a month, Becky Sue. I thought you would have come to trust me."

"It's not a matter of trust."

"Then what is it?"

She didn't reply, only continued to look at her hands that were clasped so hard her knuckles were bleached.

He noticed how her fingers trembled, and he sighed. Confronting her like this wasn't getting him anywhere. She held on to her secrets as if they were as precious as her son.

No, he corrected himself when he saw her lips trembling harder than her fingers. She was terrified. Of revealing her secrets?

He knelt by her bed. "Becky Sue, whatever or whoever frightened you and Joey was wrong. I'm here and the Waglers are here—in fact the whole *Leit* in Harmony Creek Hollow is here—to help you and your son."

"Danki," she whispered, then added nothing else.

"Whenever you're ready," he said, praying she'd have a change of heart.

God must have had other plans for them, because she stared at her folded hands and added nothing more. When Caleb stood, she didn't move.

Walking out of the room, Caleb closed the door behind him. He shook his head when Annie's worried expression voiced a question she didn't have to ask.

They had no choice but to wait for Becky Sue to be honest with them.

He hoped it would be soon, and he prayed that the teenager wouldn't take it in her head to run away with her *boppli* again.

Annie was relieved when Becky Sue agreed to join her and her siblings at the pond down the hill from the Kuhns brothers' tree farm. Moonlight shone on the snow, making it look fresh. About thirty people, including some of their *Englisch* neighbors, had come together for the evening. Annie looked forward to sampling popcorn balls and the taffy that the youth group had made.

"I guess God does love us," she said as she sat beside Caleb on a hummock where the snow had been covered with tarps and blankets.

He laughed as he laced up his skate as she did. "You sound as if this is something you've just discovered."

"I've always known it, but it's a joy to rediscover the truth over and over again. The *gut* Lord may have given us a horrible winter, but he also gave us a frozen pond to enjoy."

"I'm glad I was able to find a pair of skates in the

thrift shop by the old courthouse." Caleb pulled on his other skate after setting his boots next to each other beside the others left behind. "They had only one pair in my size."

"A skating party wouldn't be much fun without skates, ain't so?" She laced her skates with easy skill. "We had extras, so Becky Sue found a pair that fits."

"Has she said anything?"

"No." Tying off her skates, she wiggled her toes in two pairs of wool socks. "Let's not talk about that tonight."

"I agree. I hear you brought hot chocolate. Your famous recipe?"

She hoped the moonlight would wash out the blush climbing her cheeks. "I don't think it's famous."

"It should be. I've tasted your hot chocolate several times, and you add delicious flavors to it. What did you bring tonight?"

"Chocolate and raspberry."

"Is that one of the flavors you suggested serving at the bakery?"

"One of them."

"What about the others? Are they this *gut*?"

"My favorite is the chocolate and raspberry, but others prefer vanilla or the one with *kaffi* flavoring."

He slid his hand over hers as he leaned toward her. "I think we need to talk more about serving hot chocolate. Your *grossmammi* was right when she told me how many *gut* ideas you have." He finished tying his skates as he said, "Business can wait, too. Let's have fun."

When he smiled as she stood on her blades, Annie could have believed spring had erupted around them. Happiness wrapped her in warmth. Could Leanna be right? Was it possible that Caleb, a man she trusted and loved, could have strong feelings about her, too?

Caleb stood and stepped past her, gliding along the ice. She grinned. She'd learned that anything he did he did well because he gave every bit of himself to the job.

As she put her feet, one at a time, on the ice, Becky Sue skidded toward her. Annie halted her before the teen knocked them both over.

"Komm mol," called Becky Sue, holding out her hand. "Are you going to skate, or have you frozen yourself to this spot?"

With a chuckle, Annie took her hand. Becky Sue pulled her along the ice as Annie and Leanna had each other when they were little girls.

Impromptu games of snap-the-whip and races among the younger boys and girls sent waves of excited voices through the crisp winter air. Annie was pulled into some games and joined others as the evening unfolded. She waved to Caleb when she passed him as he careened across the ice after being whipped off the line of skaters. She paused once to enjoy a popcorn ball and watch as her sister skated past with Benjamin Kuhns before they fell to the ice and slid into two other people. Soon the whole crowd was laughing together.

More than once, Becky Sue came looking for her. Each time, Annie agreed to skate with the girl and used the opportunity to introduce the teen to others closer to her age.

Abruptly, Becky Sue shoved her forward. Before Annie could ask what the girl was doing, she hit something hard. Hands grabbed her arms to steady her and keep her from falling.

"You should have signal lights to show where you're going, Annie."

At Caleb's laugh, she raised her eyes to see him standing wondrously close. His chuckles faded as the heat in his eyes deepened until she feared the ice would melt under their feet. Releasing her arms, he held out his hand.

She put hers on it, and his fingers closed around it. They began to skate in perfect unison. Neither of them spoke, and that was fine. The song of their skates matched the eager beat of her heart as the other voices vanished. Every inch of her being was focused on him... on them...on being together beneath the cool moonlight as they slid along the ice while their eyes were focused on each other.

When he stopped and drew her toward the shore, she wanted to protest. He shook his head, and she followed, waiting while he ladled out two servings of her hot chocolate for them. Then, holding her hand again, he led her up the hill through the trees to a spot where they could watch the rest of the skaters.

They sipped their hot chocolate in the same silence, not needing words. When she finished the last in her paper cup, he took it and put it inside his. He set them on the ground and looked at her.

She searched his shadowed face, knowing every inch of it from the hours they'd spent together in the bakery and so many of her dreams. She closed her eyes as his arm swept around her waist and he brought her to him as he bent to caress her lips. What she'd imagined about this moment was tepid compared to the thrill of his kiss.

Did the shivers racing along her belong to him or her? All she knew for sure was that they had nothing to do with the chilly night and everything to do with the delight tingling along her. She slid her hands up the strong muscles beneath his sleeves and curved her arms over his shoulders, surrendering to the kiss she hadn't dared to believe would ever happen.

Too soon, he drew back.

Again Annie was going to protest, but she heard what he must have while she was lost in the moment.

"Hey, Caleb!" came a man's shout from closer to the pond.

Caleb leaned his forehead against hers as he murmured, "That's Lyndon. I should go and see what he wants."

"You should."

"Okay." He didn't move.

Neither did she, except to meet his mouth for another quick kiss before he picked up their discarded cups and walked awkwardly down the hill on his skates.

She remained behind, not wanting the perfection to end, wanting to keep it close so it didn't ebb away like a dream in the light of dawn. As the cold sifted through her coat and nibbled at her toes, she stood still.

Annie wasn't sure how long she remained on the hill, but her feet felt half-frozen as she lumbered down. Maybe it was time to get her skates off and put on her warm boots. A glance at the moon that was setting over the mountains to the west told her that the party had been going on for more than two hours.

A clump of shadows in front of her were, she discovered as she drew near, a group of men leaning on the trees and sipping her hot chocolate. She was about to announce herself when she caught Caleb's voice.

"The plan is to have a full selection of drink choices." He laughed, "*Englischers* are always talking about taking time to stop and smell the roses. Maybe we can convince them to stop and smell the *kaffi* and the hot chocolate and maybe freshly squeezed lemonade in the summer. I've been looking around to find some more small tables. If they're set in one corner, we hope patrons will stay and have something to eat before they take more home with them."

"That's a *gut* idea." Her brother slapped Caleb's arm. "A really *gut* one. You've put a lot of thought into this."

Another man spoke. An *Englischer*. "I can tell that you've done your market research, Caleb. We've needed a café and a bakery in Salem since the last one was turned into a diner a few years ago." He paused, then said, "My wife will be your best customer, I'm sure, once she tastes this raspberry hot chocolate. She raves about the bread you sold last summer. That you'll be serving hot drinks at a place where she can get together with her friends will make her really happy."

"You'll get a bunch of guys in there before evening chores, too," said another *Englischer*. Chief Pulaski, Annie realized, as the fire chief continued, "I shouldn't be surprised that you've got so many good ideas. Your suggestion about having that Amish-style mud sale raised enough money to pay for a lot of training for our volunteers."

"Danki."

"Your bakery is sure to be a hit. When I was in to do the final inspection this morning, I couldn't believe the transformation of that dusty old depot into a bright and cheery shop. How did you come up with the idea of splashing color on the floor? I thought you Amish liked things plain."

She waited, holding her breath because she didn't want to miss a single word. *Now* Caleb would say some of the ideas had been hers.

"We do." He chuckled. "But when my cousin's little boy spilled paint, it seemed like the obvious solution when it would have taken so long to clean up those old floorboards."

"And that bright yellow wall in the kitchen?" Chief Pulaski chuckled. "I'd guess I won't be the only husband in Salem who'll be repainting a kitchen once your shop opens."

"When customers come in, the color of that wall will catch their attention. That will draw their eyes right to the displays in the cases."

Annie reeled a half step as she heard what she'd said, almost word for word, coming out of Caleb's mouth. He was taking credit for her ideas as Rolan had after they'd broken up. How could she have been foolish enough to let this happen again? She'd thought Caleb cared about her, but had he cared only about the ideas she brought him for his bakery?

Stop it! she told herself. It shouldn't matter who got credit for how the bakery had turned out. To expect to be acknowledged for her help was *hochmut*. She should be pleased that her hard work was paying off for Caleb.

But how could she when he'd taken her ideas for his own?

She should have been more careful. If she hadn't let flattery from her *grossmammi* and from Caleb turn her head, she might have thought before she let each idea burst out of her. Instead, she'd freed each one as it popped into her mind, so glad to be able to express them.

And the worst part was that he didn't seem to have any problem with taking credit for her ideas mere minutes after he'd wooed her lips with his. Rolan hadn't tried to keep her off-kilter like that when he stole her ideas.

Bending over, Annie loosened the laces on her skates. She tramped through the snow to where she'd left her boots. She yanked off her skates and pulled on her boots. She looked around and saw Leanna and Becky Sue talking to Juanita and Kenny a short distance away.

"Let's go," Annie said as she approached them.

"But, Annie—"

She didn't give Becky Sue a chance to finish. Linking her arm through the teenager's, she marched toward the road that twisted through the hollow. A glance back told her that her siblings were hurrying to follow and that Caleb was striding in their direction.

Talking to him would be another mistake. If she did, she might say something she'd come to regret later.

She shot another look over her shoulder. Caleb had stopped, staring after them. Puzzlement was seared on his face.

He doesn't realize what he's done.

That thought should have been comforting.

It wasn't.

Her pain was too deep, her betrayal too raw. She couldn't think about the situation logically.

What a joke! Annie Wagler, the always-logical one, the twin who didn't lead with her emotions but worked well with everyone, was the one who refused to listen to her own rational thoughts. Instead she was wallowing in pain, a pain so deep it hurt to breathe.

No one spoke on the short walk home. Her younger sister and brother glanced at her again and again, but apparently the set of her taut lips told them it'd be wise not to ask questions. They and Becky Sue hurried up to their rooms, and she could hear the soft buzz of their confused voices.

Leanna stayed in the kitchen and watched as Annie tried to find something to do to vent her frustration.

After about fifteen minutes, she took Annie by the arm and steered her to the table.

"What's going on?" Leanna asked.

"Caleb Hartz isn't the man I thought he was." The words sprang out of her like soda from a shaken bottle.

Her twin frowned and tapped her foot on the floor. "I'm not going to ask you what happened between you, but I can tell you that pouting about it and going around crashing into things and cutting short the *kinder*'s fun won't change it."

"I'm not doing anything different from what you've been doing."

"Me?" Her twin looked shocked.

"*Ja.* You've been in mourning since Gabriel Miller got married."

Leanna recoiled as if Annie had struck her. "I have not!"

"You don't see it, but you've been acting as if you're attending a wake for months and months. You used to laugh and sing and delight in making your quilts. I don't think I've heard you sing, other than during services, in a year. Each time you pick up a needle, you act as if quilting is drudgery instead of the joy it used to be. You enjoy taking care of your goats, but you've handed the job to me a lot lately. It's as if you've forgotten how to be happy."

Her twin stared at Annie. More than once, she opened her mouth to speak, but didn't break the silence that clamped around them.

Leanna threw her arms around Annie. "I'm sorry. I have been so focused on what I didn't have that I've forgotten what I do have. I've been selfish and let you carry too much of the load of moving here and watching over the others. My sole excuse is that you do everything so well that I've been going along with whatever you say and do."

"I don't do everything well." She'd made a mess of her relationship with Caleb.

She admitted to herself what scared her most: that, after tonight, they couldn't even be friends any longer.

Chapter Sixteen

It was quiet.

Too quiet.

The last time Caleb had been smothered by such silence at the bakery was the day before he hired Annie to work for him. Since then, the space had been alive with her *gut* humor and lively questions and endless suggestions aimed at helping him make his dream come true.

It was coming true, but at what price? Last night, Annie had stormed away from the pond without explaining why she was upset. He'd stopped by the Waglers' house earlier to pick her up. Leanna had met him on the porch and informed him Annie wouldn't be coming to work that day.

"How about tomorrow?" he'd asked.

Leanna had deflected his question, and he'd realized he wasn't going to get a straight answer. Unwilling to storm into the house and demand Annie explain—though the idea was tempting—he'd thanked Leanna, got into his buggy and headed toward the bakery.

But the silence taunted him. The bright colors on the floor and the shining appliances and display cases were mute reminders of how hard she'd worked by his side.

Now she didn't want to see him.

Like Verba when he didn't do as she wanted. She'd dumped him because she told him that she was tired of being less important to him than his dream of a successful bakery. Had he made the same mistake again? No. Verba had ended their courtship because he refused to become the man she wanted for a husband, a man who met each of her very precise specifications.

After that, he'd vowed to himself and to God that he'd never put himself in such a situation again. And he hadn't, had he?

No, he hadn't.

Annie was, he realized with a start, the complete opposite of Verba. Instead of trying to change him, Annie had spent hours coming up with ideas to make his dream better than he could have devised on his own. She'd accepted his hopes for his future as if they were as integral a part of him as his hair color and his faith.

She'd enhanced those dreams, caring about them as much as if they were her own.

Every time he'd needed her help—even when he hadn't known he could use her assistance—she'd stepped up and offered to do what she could. It hadn't mattered that what she volunteered to do added to her already heavy burden of taking care of her family and their farm. She'd smiled and taken over the task and done it well.

Better than he could have many times.

Would he have thought about the color on the kitchen wall and how it would draw customers' eyes to his baked goods on display in the front room?

Would he ever have conceived the idea of putting tables and chairs in the open space to one side of the display case so people would buy extra *kaffi*, other drinks and extra sweets from him? And turning the *boppli*'s splattering of paint on the floor from a disaster to something fun never would have entered his mind.

The bakery seemed like a dead thing. Annie was gone, and he didn't know why. Because he'd kissed her last night? He'd thought she was willing when she stepped into his arms. She must have had second thoughts after their kiss, but why hadn't she told him? She'd been honest about so much else, even when he hadn't liked her honesty.

Caleb flinched when he heard a knock on the door. Who could be there? He didn't want to see some chirpy salesman or curious neighbor. He wanted to be alone with his misery.

With a sigh, he went to the door and opened it. He didn't recognize the lanky teenager who stood in front of him. The lad was overdue for a haircut because dark bangs covered his eyes. He was dressed in plain clothing, though it wasn't the style worn in their district.

"Gute mariye," Caleb said.

The young man shuffled his worn boots. "My name is Elson Knepp. I'm looking for Becky Sue Hartz, and I've been told I might find her or her cousin Caleb here."

"I'm Caleb Hartz. Why are you looking for Becky Sue?"

The young man ducked his head, then squared his shoulders and looked Caleb in the eye. "Because she's going to be my wife. We've got plans to build a life and a family together."

"Aren't you a bit late for that?"

Elson's brow threaded with confusion, and then dismay dimmed his eyes. "Late? Are you telling me that she's decided to marry someone else?"

"No, I'm telling you that she already has a family."

"Do you mean her family in Lancaster County?" His

lip curled. "That's no family for her." His brows rose. "Or do you mean her cousins here? I'm not sure what you're trying to tell me."

Caleb scowled. "I'm trying to tell you that Becky Sue already has a family. She and her *boppli* are a family."

The young man swayed on his feet as he grew ashen.

Putting out a hand, because he feared Elson was about to faint, Caleb guided the younger man toward the tables he'd brought to the bakery. He took down a stacked chair and helped Elson sit.

"Do you want something to drink?" Caleb asked.

"No. I…" Elson's voice drifted away.

"Are you okay?"

"Did you say Becky Sue—Becky Sue Hartz—has a *boppli*? That I'm a *daed*?"

It was Caleb's turn to be shocked. He wasn't sure what plain community Elson was from, but he did know that the young man wasn't an *Englischer*. Even if one had decided to put on plain clothes and give himself a plain name, he couldn't speak *Deitsch* with the ease of someone who'd always used it.

But Becky Sue had told Annie that Joey's *daed* was *Englisch*. Hadn't she? Or had she just implied that? Was it all another lie? Caleb was determined to find out.

After convincing the young man to have a cup of *kaffi* to warm him, though Caleb suspected shock more than the outside temperatures had more to do with Elson's shivering, Caleb got another chair and sat facing him.

"Start from the beginning," Caleb said as he stirred cream into his *kaffi* and watched Elson add several spoonfuls of sugar to his own cup.

"Becky Sue and I walked out together, and we discovered we loved each other and wanted to spend the rest of our lives together. She wasn't happy at home because her stepfather made her life miserable."

"Stepfather? I didn't know she had one."

"Her own *daed*'s brother, which is why they have the same last name, but he made it clear soon after his first son was born that he wished she didn't exist. He favored his own *kinder* over her. If money was tight, she was the last one to get new shoes or a coat that fitted. She and I agreed it would be for the best if we got married as soon as possible. I didn't have enough money to provide for us, so I took a job in Iowa. Out there, they need workers and don't ask a lot of questions." He flushed, his face becoming tomato red. "The night before I left, we... That is..."

Caleb took pity on the young man. "You don't have to go into detail. You and Becky Sue aren't the first to make that bad decision, and you won't be the last. Have you been in Iowa all this time?" He thought of the phone number with an Iowan area code that had been made before Annie and he had found Becky Sue at the bakery.

Had she been trying to get in touch with Elson so he'd know where she and his son were?

A rush of anger swept through him as he wondered how any man, even one as wet behind the ears as Elson, could abandon his family. Then he paused. Elson seemed genuinely shocked. Was it possible the young man hadn't known about his son?

"Caleb," the teenager said as if Caleb had asked that question aloud, "you've got to believe me. I wanted to earn enough money so I could provide for us. I love Becky Sue, but I had no idea when I left for Iowa that Becky Sue was pregnant. I wouldn't have left her by herself, if I'd known. There could have been other ways to earn enough to provide for her and me and the *boppli* right there in Lancaster County."

"Did you let her know where you were?"

"I wrote to her every other day right from the beginning, but she seldom wrote back. I'd get a letter from her about once a month. They were short."

"But you talked on the phone."

Again Elson shook his head. "Never, though as soon as I got a cell phone in Iowa, I sent her my number and urged her to call me collect. I missed hearing her voice and her laughter. I fell in love with her because of her laugh. Silly, ain't so?"

Caleb sighed. "No, it's not." Annie's laugh created special music in his soul.

Elson hung his head as he clenched his hands by his sides. "She never called, and she never wrote to me about being pregnant or having a *boppli*."

Though Caleb wanted to say that was hard to believe, he thought of how habit-forming secrets could be. He hadn't revealed to Annie anything about how Verba had shamed him…how he'd allowed her to make him question everything he held dear. And Annie hid something from him, something he could sense when he kissed her, but he couldn't guess what it was.

"Are she and the *boppli* okay?"

"They are. They're staying with friends of mine." At least, he hoped he could still say Annie was his friend. "Becky Sue is doing well, and so is Joey, though he has trouble seeing."

"Joey? I have a son?" Joy brought color to Elson's cheeks.

Looking at him, Caleb knew there was no doubt that the young man was being truthful. Becky Sue had kept him in the dark, never telling him that she had his *kind*.

"*Komm* with me," he said, getting up. He couldn't let his and Annie's problems get in the way of Elson meeting his son. He wasn't sure what reception he'd get at the Waglers, but he'd wait outside if he had to. Nothing must prevent a reunion between Becky Sue, Elson and their son.

"What is wrong with you today?" chided Becky Sue as she bent to pick up the pieces of the second cup Annie had dropped while they did the breakfast dishes together. "Is something wrong with you and Caleb?"

Annie shook her head. "No, there isn't any Caleb and me."

"But I thought…" Becky Sue looked to Leanna as she added, "I thought by now you two were walking out together."

"I worked for him. Nothing more."

"No! Don't be false to us!" Leanna snapped.

"I told you last night—"

"You didn't tell me anything. You changed the subject to how I felt about Gabriel marrying someone else. You said Caleb wasn't the man you thought he was. That could mean anything. Anything at all!" Leanna stamped her foot, shocking Annie, who couldn't remember the last time her twin had been so assertive. "You can lie to yourself, but you've got to be honest to me, Annie. It's no more than you asked of me when you tried to make a match for me with Caleb."

Embarrassment heated her face. She *had* insisted that Leanna speak from the heart with her after attending the mud sale with Caleb.

"I worked so hard," Becky Sue groaned. "I knew you liked him and he liked you. When you were *dumm* enough to fix up Leanna with him, I decided you must be shown how wrong you are. Both of you."

Comprehension burst into Annie's mind. "When you locked us in the closet?"

"*Ja.* I hid in your horrible cellar beneath the trap door until you both went into the closet to get the dishwasher detergent I'd moved. When that didn't seem to convince you that you're right for each other, I *disappeared.*" She made air quotes. "It seemed to work, but then you'd get busy and I wasn't sure you were making time for each other. I came up with an idea to get you to spend time together." She glanced at the sleeping *boppli.* "Joey helped me that time."

"With all the paint mess?" Annie had had no idea that the teenager was so ingenious.

Becky Sue had taken advantage of the few tools she had to throw Annie and Caleb together, and she'd succeeded each time. At least for a while, until one of them stepped away, unsure about what their relationship might have become.

"And you kissed him last night," Becky Sue cried. "How could you do that if you don't like him?"

"You were spying on us?"

The girl didn't deny the accusation. "If you two can't see the truth, someone has to help you."

Annie threw the dish towel on the counter and turned to leave the kitchen. She paused when the door opened.

Her eyes widened, but her heart beat out a joyous song when Caleb stepped in. Her tears distorted his image, but his handsome face had been etched into her memory so she could recreate each angle as if he stood in the brightest sunshine. She looked away, startled when Becky Sue gasped before she said words almost identical to the ones Caleb had used the day they found her and Joey at the bakery.

"Elson, what are you doing *here*?"

A lanky young man she didn't know rushed into the kitchen and tugged Becky Sue into his arms. He buried his face in the side of her *kapp* as he kept repeating her name over and over. She pointed to the *boppli*, who was rousing with the uproar.

"Elson," she whispered, "there's your son. Our son."

Unabashed tears ran down the young man's face, and Annie's heart pushed aside the last of the wall she'd built around it. Here was true joy, the reunion of two hearts that belonged together. No matter what she did, she couldn't have found this for her sister. Only Leanna, with God's help, could find it for herself.

Grossmammi Inez tiptoed into the kitchen, putting a finger to her lips because she didn't want her arrival to disrupt what was happening.

"I'm sorry I wasn't honest with you, Caleb and the rest of you." Becky Sue looked toward Elson as she picked up Joey and cuddled him close. "I couldn't be honest with anyone else when I wasn't honest with myself. I thought you'd be better off without me…without us."

"How could you believe that?" Elson took a step toward her, then halted. "Or was it that you thought you were better off without *me*? I know your parents never liked me."

"Leo Hartz is not my parent, so I don't care what he thought. He's just the man my *mamm* married after my real *daed* died, and he always has let me know that he wished she hadn't had a daughter before they wedded. I was told I should call him by his given name while his *kinder* called him *daed*."

Annie drew in a sharp breath, trying to imagine her

own *mamm*'s second husband treating her and Leanna and Lyndon cruelly. Bert Wagler had treated the three of them as he had his own son and daughter. He was the person she thought of when talking about her *daed* because her own had sickened when she was so young.

Becky Sue turned to Caleb. "I should have told you why Joey was scared of you. It's because you have similar coloring to Leo. From the day he was born, Joey has known that Leo wished he didn't exist. I tried to keep Joey away from him, but Leo yelled at Joey about the slightest thing. I know he hit Joey, too, though I never caught him doing it."

He put a hand on her shoulder. "I'm sorry to hear that, Becky Sue. And I'm sorry that I believed there was no *gut* reason for you to run away. I was wrong."

Tears glistened in the girl's eyes, and this time she didn't try to hold them in. "*Danki*, Caleb. I've wanted you to understand, but I wasn't sure if you'd listen when nobody else had."

"Though you came here for sanctuary."

"I'd heard from so many people what a *gut* guy you were."

"But you still couldn't trust me."

"No, because while I hoped you'd help me—and you did—I've been afraid that, if I told you the truth, you'd tell me the same thing others did." She blinked on more tears. "When I sought help from our ministers, they told me that while Joey and I lived with Leo, I had to heed his rules. They thought I was a disgruntled stepdaughter who was looking to cause trouble." Thick teardrops fell onto her apron. "I had been that girl when I was Kenny's age because I didn't know how to put in the proper words what was happening at our house." She looked up at him again. "I got the punishments I deserved, but Joey didn't do anything wrong other than being born."

"And even that wasn't his choice," Elson said as he put his arm around her.

"But you're happy about it, ain't so?" the girl asked, sounding younger.

"Happier than you can know. As soon as we can become baptized, I want us to marry and have a real family. The three of us to begin with and whoever God sends to us after that."

She handed him his son, telling him to hold Joey close to his face. When the *boppli* ran inquisitive hands along Elson's features, Becky Sue whispered, "This is *Daed*, Joey. *Daed*."

"Daed?" the little boy asked.

"Ja," Elson whispered. "And you are my dear, dear son."

Annie's eyes overflowed as she watched the family that had been separated for so long come together. She doubted anything on earth would pull them apart again, because Becky Sue stared at Elson as if she could never get enough of looking at him. And the young man did the same to her.

When a hand took hers, tugging her toward the door, she knew it belonged to Caleb. There was a sense, a sense with no name, that connected them in a way she'd never imagined. She was sure a storm raged along her skin that prickled as if she'd stood too close to a lightning bolt.

"Will you talk to me?" he whispered as he opened the door to the mud room.

She steeled herself against the cold, but how could that bother her when his touch was so warm?

"Ja," she whispered, unable to speak more loudly.

He turned her so they stood face-to-face as they had on the hill overlooking the pond. "I don't know what I did wrong, Annie, but I'm sorry. I don't ever want to do anything to hurt you."

"You have to understand what happened in the past." As she told him how Rolan had betrayed her, she saw anger spark in his eyes. Not at her, but at the man who'd used her so. "Last night, I heard…that is, I thought I heard while you were talking to Lyndon and your firefighter friends…"

"That I took credit for your ideas? That I let them think they were my ideas?" He framed her face with his work-worn hands. "If I did, it was by mistake."

"I know you're not like Rolan because you've been eager to make use of my ideas and include me, not steal them for yourself."

He thought for a few seconds, then asked, "Are you sure I let the others think the ideas were mine? I remember saying 'we' because we've worked together on the bakery."

Annie stepped away so she could think. She replayed the conversation she'd overheard—or as much as she could remember, examining every word. In amazement, she realized he was right. He hadn't let the others assume the ideas were his. In fact, he'd gone out of his way to avoid that. Her perceptions had led her to believe otherwise.

"How did you know I cared so much about my ideas?" she asked.

"Because I care that much about my dreams, and when someone tried to stand in my way, telling me those dreams were useless, I ended what I thought we shared."

"You did?"

"Ja." He took her hands and laced his fingers through hers. "I've made a lot of mistakes, Annie, but there's one I'll never make again."

"What's that?"

"Not knowing if I was talking to you or Leanna." He lifted her right hand and pressed it to the center of his chest. "My heart will always be sure. It wants to belong to you, if you'll have it."

"Only if you take mine," she laughed. "Not that you have any choice. It refuses *not* to belong to you. *Ich liebe dich*, Caleb."

"And I love you, too. I want us to be partners in life as well as working at the bakery. Will you marry me?"

She flung her arms around his shoulders and answered him with a kiss. When she heard excited shouts behind her, she looked over her shoulder to see her family and his clustered in the doorway.

"I guess you've heard," Caleb said with a chuckle.

"We haven't heard her say *ja*," *Grossmammi* Inez replied.

"Ja!" Annie repeated about a half-dozen times until she and everyone else dissolved into laughter.

Caleb held up one finger. "However, I want you to witness that there's one more promise I need to hear Annie make."

"What's that?" she asked.

"That you'll like milking cows."

She laughed, "That's never going to happen."

"Never is a long time, Annie."

"How about this? I'll let you try to convince me for the rest of our lives."

"That sounds like a *wunderbaar* plan."

Epilogue

"Ready?" Caleb asked as he held out his left hand. In his right, he held a tray of apple pie squares. It would claim the last empty spot in the display cases.

"Ready." Annie smiled at him as she clasped his hand.

They walked together out of the kitchen and into the front room of the bakery. Everything glistened in the warm morning sunshine pouring through the pristine windows. The light danced on the quartet of black tables topped with containers of creamers and sugar, waiting for customers to sit and enjoy a cup of *kaffi*. It sparkled on the glass in the display cases and across the small refrigerator Caleb had installed the day before when they realized they wanted to have a place to store fresh milk, cream and whipped cream for the drinks and baked goods.

Yesterday, she'd joined him out front when he installed the sign that announced Hartz Bakery would soon be open for business. She treasured the memory of his smile when he finished patting down the dirt around the posts holding the sign in place. His dream was coming true, and so was hers.

She looked at the multicolored floorboards. A smile tilted her lips as it did each time she thought of the little boy and his *mamm* and *daed*, who had decided to remain in Harmony Creek Hollow. They were renting a small tenant house from the Bowmans, whose farm was about halfway between Caleb's house and Miriam's. Joey had been seen by a *doktor* who had several ideas for helping him see better. Elson had already begun work with her friend Sarah's brothers at their sawmill, and he and Becky Sue were attending baptism classes. A happy ending to a difficult story...

And Annie was relieved that her *grossmammi* was going to see a cardiac specialist next week. She prayed the *doktor* would be able to diagnosis what was causing *Grossmammi* Inez to be so short of breath.

"You look happy," Caleb said after placing the tray in the display case.

"How can I not be happy? Becky Sue and Joey are being taken care of and your bakery is opening today."

"*Our* bakery." He ran his fingers along her cheek. "I didn't realize how much better a dream coming true could be when it was a dream shared."

"As I didn't know that once an idea is brought to life, it can belong to both of us."

He glanced toward the window where a line snaked from the door all the way around the driveway. With a husky laugh, he pulled her to him and gave her a resounding kiss that sent delight racing from her lips to the very tips of her toes. He drew back enough to whisper, "We'll finish the kiss later."

"And start more."

Chuckling, he squeezed her. "I love how you think." He released her and walked to the door.

Annie positioned herself behind the counter where

she'd take the orders from their customers. When he looked at her, she gave him a thumbs-up.

He threw the door open and said, with a flourish of his arm, "Welcome to the Hartz Bakery."

A cheer rose from outside, and Annie almost shivered with glee. Their hard work had brought this day. Not just working on the bakery, but the tougher task of learning to trust each other after being betrayed in the past.

Checking that her *kapp* hadn't shifted while she helped Caleb put the goods in the cases, she greeted their very first customer, "*Gute mariye*, Deputy Flanagan. What can I get for you today?"

The tall man selected two raspberry muffins and three oatmeal-raisin cookies. As Annie put them into a small box, she looked past the deputy to where Caleb was talking with some of his fellow firefighters who were waiting for their turn to place their orders. He smiled at her, and she wondered how her heart could hold so much happiness as his dream and her own came true. She had a lifetime with him to figure that out.

* * * * *

Dear Reader,

We all have dreams. I have had the dream of being a published author since I was twelve years old. Each time I have another book published, it's like that dream coming true all over again.

But we have to balance those dreams with the real world. Both have to be equally important, or our dreams can end up dead and useless. On the other hand, some dreams aren't meant to come true, as Annie has to learn. Isn't it splendid that usually when that happens, we find, as both Caleb and Annie do, that God had a plan all along for us that leads us to new and better dreams?

Visit me at www.joannbrownbooks.com. Look for the final story in the Amish Spinster Club series, coming soon.

Wishing you many blessings,
Jo Ann Brown

Get 4 FREE REWARDS!

We'll send you 2 FREE Books plus <u>plus</u> 2 FREE Mystery Gifts.

Love Inspired® books feature contemporary inspirational romances with Christian characters facing the challenges of life and love.

FREE Value Over **$20**

YES! Please send me 2 FREE Love Inspired® Romance novels and my 2 FREE mystery gifts (gifts are worth about $10 retail). After receiving them, if I don't wish to receive any more books, I can return the shipping statement marked "cancel." If I don't cancel, I will receive 6 brand-new novels every month and be billed just $5.24 for the regular-print edition or $5.74 each for the larger-print edition in the U.S., or $5.74 each for the regular-print edition or $6.24 each for the larger-print edition in Canada. That's a savings of at least 13% off the cover price. It's quite a bargain! Shipping and handling is just 50¢ per book in the U.S. and 75¢ per book in Canada.* I understand that accepting the 2 free books and gifts places me under no obligation to buy anything. I can always return a shipment and cancel at any time. The free books and gifts are mine to keep no matter what I decide.

Choose one: ☐ **Love Inspired® Romance**
Regular-Print
(105/305 IDN GMY4)

☐ **Love Inspired® Romance**
Larger-Print
(122/322 IDN GMY4)

Name (please print)

Address   Apt. #

City   State/Province   Zip/Postal Code

Mail to the **Reader Service:**
IN U.S.A.: P.O. Box 1341, Buffalo, NY 14240-8531
IN CANADA: P.O. Box 603, Fort Erie, Ontario L2A 5X3

Want to try 2 free books from another series? Call 1-800-873-8635 or visit www.ReaderService.com.

---

*Terms and prices subject to change without notice. Prices do not include sales taxes, which will be charged (if applicable) based on your state or country of residence. Canadian residents will be charged applicable taxes. Offer not valid in Quebec. This offer is limited to one order per household. Books received may not be as shown. Not valid for current subscribers to Love Inspired Romance books. All orders subject to approval. Credit or debit balances in a customer's account(s) may be offset by any other outstanding balance owed by or to the customer. Please allow 4 to 6 weeks for delivery. Offer available while quantities last.

Your Privacy—The Reader Service is committed to protecting your privacy. Our Privacy Policy is available online at www.ReaderService.com or upon request from the Reader Service. We make a portion of our mailing list available to reputable third parties that offer products we believe may interest you. If you prefer that we not exchange your name with third parties, or if you wish to clarify or modify your communication preferences, please visit us at www.ReaderService.com/consumerchoice or write to us at Reader Service Preference Service, P.O. Box 9062, Buffalo, NY 14240-9062. Include your complete name and address.

LI19R

*Read on for a sneak peek at
the first heartwarming book in Lee Tobin McClain's
Safe Haven series,* Low Country Hero*!*

They'd both just turned back to their work when a familiar loud, croaking sound cut the silence.

The twins shrieked and ran from where they'd been playing into the little cabin's yard and slammed into Anna, their faces frightened.

"What was that?" Anna sounded alarmed, too, kneeling to hold and comfort both girls.

"Nothing to be afraid of," Sean said, trying to hold back laughter. "It's just egrets. Type of water bird." He located the source of the sound, then went over to the trio, knelt beside them, and pointed through the trees and growth.

When the girls saw the stately white birds, they gasped.

"They're so pretty!" Anna said.

"Pretty?" Sean chuckled. "Nobody from around here would get excited about an egret, nor think it's especially pretty." But as he watched another one land beside the first, white wings spread wide as it skidded into the shallow water, he realized that there was beauty there. He just hadn't noticed it before.

That was what kids did for you: made you see the world through their fresh, innocent eyes. A fist of longing clutched inside his chest.

The twins were tugging at Anna's shirt now, trying to get her to take them over toward the birds. "You may go look as long as you can see me," she said, "but take careful steps by the water." She took the bolder twin's face in her hands. "The water's not deep, but I still don't want you to wade in. Do you understand?"

Both little girls nodded vigorously.

They ran off and she watched for a few seconds, then turned back to her work with a barely audible sigh.

"Go take a look with them," he urged her. "It's not every day kids see an egret for the first time."

"You're sure?"

"Go on." He watched her run like a kid over to her girls. And then he couldn't resist walking a few steps closer and watching them, shielded by the trees and brush.

The twins were so excited that they weren't remembering to be quiet. "It caught a *fish*!" the one was crowing, pointing at the bird, which, indeed, held a squirming fish in its mouth.

"That one's neck is like an S!" The quieter twin squatted down, rapt.

Anna eased down onto the sandy beach, obviously unworried about her or the girls getting wet or dirty, laughing and talking to them and sharing their excitement.

The sight of it gave him a melancholy twinge. His own mom had been a nature lover. She'd taken him and his brothers fishing, visited a nature reserve a few times, back in Alabama where they'd lived before coming here.

Oh, if things were different, he'd run with this, see where it led…

Don't miss
Lee Tobin McClain's Low Country Hero,
available March 2019 from HQN Books!

www.Harlequin.com

PHLTMEXP0319